On the Trail of Trouble

"Easy, boy," Nancy cooed to the horse.

"What's happening?" George called.

"My horse won't get near that pile of rubble," Nancy said.

They both heard the sound at the same time. It started soft and slow, then grew loud and very fast. Nancy saw the snake first, almost camouflaged in the wreckage. It was a thick, mottled coil with a tapering head in the center. At the end of its tail, a small brown rattle shook with menace.

Nancy could feel her horse's heart beating as she tried to calm him. Her own heart was pounding just as fast.

Suddenly—as if it were on a spring—the snake shot forward.

Nancy Drew
Mystery Stories

#104 The Mystery of the Jade Tiger
#108 The Secret of the Tibetan Treasure
#110 The Nutcracker Ballet Mystery
#112 Crime in the Queen's Court
#116 The Case of the Twin Teddy Bears
#119 The Mystery of the Missing Mascot
#120 The Case of the Floating Crime
#125 The Teen Model Mystery
#126 The Riddle in the Rare Book
#127 The Case of the Dangerous Solution
#128 The Treasure in the Royal Tower
#129 The Baby-sitter Burglaries
#130 The Sign of the Falcon
#132 The Fox Hunt Mystery
#133 The Mystery at the Crystal Palace

#134 The Secret of the Forgotten Cave
#135 The Riddle of the Ruby Gazelle
#136 The Wedding Day Mystery
#137 In Search of the Black Rose
#138 The Legend of the Lost Gold
#139 The Secret of Candlelight Inn
#140 The Door-to-Door Deception
#141 The Wild Cat Crime
#142 The Case of Capital Intrigue
#143 Mystery on Maui
#144 The E-mail Mystery
#145 The Missing Horse Mystery
#146 The Ghost of the Lantern Lady
#147 The Case of the Captured Queen
#148 On the Trail of Trouble

Available from MINSTREL Books

NANCY DREW® 148

ON THE
TRAIL OF TROUBLE

CAROLYN KEENE

A MINSTREL® BOOK

Published by POCKET BOOKS
New York   London   Toronto   Sydney   Tokyo   Singapore

A MINSTREL PAPERBACK *Original*

A Minstrel Book published by
POCKET BOOKS, a division of Simon & Schuster, Inc.
1230 Avenue of the Americas, New York, NY 10020

ISBN: 0-671-02664-X

First Minstrel Books printing March 1999

10 9 8 7 6 5 4 3 2 1

NANCY DREW, NANCY DREW MYSTERY STORIES,
A MINSTREL BOOK and colophon are registered
trademarks of Simon & Schuster, Inc.

Cover art by Ernie Norcia

Printed in the U.S.A.

Contents

1   Where Is Justice?   1
2   Rattled!   11
3   A Chilling Call   20
4   The Jawbone Talks   29
5   A Reflection of Danger   41
6   The Puzzle Deepens   51
7   A Mountain Menace   61
8   Bess Tumbles for Lincoln   73
9   A Few Pieces Fit   82
10 Bad Times at the Badlands   90
11 Braving the Badger's Lair   99
12 More Pieces Turn Up   108
13 Peril in the Pines   118
14 Finding the Mother Lode   129
15 All the Pieces Fit   139

ON THE
TRAIL OF TROUBLE

1

Where Is Justice?

Nancy Drew looked out over the rolling hills of pasture. In the distance she could see a herd of huge brown animals walking slowly through the green and gold grass. Behind them, jagged mountain peaks cut into the horizon. "They have the best profile of any animal ever," she said.

"I love their legs," Nancy's friend George Fayne said. Leaning against the corral fence, she held up a hand to shield her brown eyes from the South Dakota sun. "Buffalo have these humongous heads and bodies, but such skinny legs."

"But those legs are super strong," came a voice behind them. "They can run at thirty-five miles an hour for a half hour straight. That's faster than a

1

horse and rider at top speed." Nancy and George turned to greet their hostess, Kincaid Turner. "Bess will be here in a minute," Kincaid added. "She wanted to change her sweater."

"Typical," George muttered. "We got here an hour ago, and Bess has already changed clothes twice."

Bess Marvin was George's cousin, even though they were physical opposites. George was tall, slim, and athletic, with dark hair and eyes. Bess was shorter with a fuller figure, and she had straw blond hair and pale blue eyes.

"I heard that," Bess called out as she joined them. "And they're not buffalo," she added, lightly jabbing George with her elbow. "They're bison. Right, Kincaid?"

"Strictly speaking, you're correct," Kincaid said with a laugh. She had a pretty face, with a cap of light brown hair and bangs. She was tall with long slim legs. Nancy figured she was about eighteen— the same age as Nancy and her friends.

"Real buffalo live in Asia and Africa, and they don't look like these guys at all," Bess continued. "But people have been calling American bison *buffalo* for so long, it's become their other name. Even the locals call them buffalo." She gestured to the small sign over the corral: M-Bar-B Buffalo Ranch.

"I'm impressed," Kincaid said. "You were paying attention after all."

"Hey, I learned a lot from all those times I've visited here," Bess said. "I'm so happy Nancy and George could come this time even though the circumstances aren't the best."

"I am, too," Kincaid said. "I sure hope you can help us, Nancy." Kincaid looked so upset that Nancy thought she might burst into tears. Then Kincaid took a deep breath and clenched her hands into fists. "This is just tearing up my folks. We've got to catch the rustlers soon or we'll be out of business."

"Don't worry," Bess said, putting an arm around Kincaid's shoulder. "Nancy will figure this out. She's the best."

Kincaid led them through the corral that surrounded the area at the front of the huge barn. "Bess said you've already lost thirty animals," Nancy said. She shook her head and brushed strands of reddish blond hair out of her bright blue eyes.

"That was last week," Kincaid said. "Ten more disappeared a couple of days ago. Dad's out now with some hands moving the herd in closer."

"Closer?" George asked.

"Usually, we let them have the run of our thousand acres," Kincaid said.

"Wow," Nancy said, impressed by the size of the ranch.

"We have over three hundred head of bison. Even on a thousand acres there's not enough wild oats, rye, and grass to keep that many bison happy. So we also give them feedlot supplement," Kincaid explained. "Now with all the rustling, Dad has to bring the herd in closer and build new fence so we can keep them nearer to the ranchhouse compound. This means we'll have to give them more feedlot supplement, which costs money."

As they entered the barn, they heard a huge bellowing roar echo from the distance. "Was that a mountain lion?" George asked.

"Nope," Kincaid said, her golden brown eyes twinkling with amusement. "Just one of the bulls from our herd showing off."

"The corral has a wood fence," Nancy said. "But what about the fence around your ranch itself, around the thousand acres of pasture. What's it made of?"

"Wire," Kincaid said. "For horses or cattle you need a fence five feet high. For bison, it has to be eight feet. The top few rows of wire are barbed. The lower rows aren't."

"What are the rustlers getting out of this?" Nancy asked. "How much are buffalo—bison— worth?"

"Just say buffalo," Kincaid said, smiling. "We switch back and forth between the two names. A two-year-old is worth at least sixteen hundred dollars. Good breeding stock can be worth more."

"I was here when a calf named Lulu was born," Bess said. "She was unbelievable—a rusty brown color. She looked like a fifty-pound cinnamon ball.

4

Kincaid hand-raised her and showed her in exhibitions and competitions—she was a real pet."

"You won't believe it, but she's a mother now," Kincaid said.

"Wow!" Bess answered.

"She had a calf herself a few weeks ago," Kincaid added. "I named him Justice after my grandfather. I'm going to raise him as I did her. Lulu's still real tame, and she's wonderful."

"Where are they?" Bess said. "I'd love to see them. Do you think she'll remember me?"

"Probably," Kincaid said. "She's really smart. I have them in one of my secret places, isolated from the rest of the herd. Cows like to keep to themselves when they give birth, and I want to keep Justice safe for a few more weeks. Don't want him to get bumped or bruised. We'll ride out to see them after lunch."

The girls spent the rest of the morning touring the ranch. Then they went back to the house for lunch. "This is the best hamburger I've ever had, Mrs. Turner," George said, after swallowing her first bite.

"Actually, it's a buffalo burger," Mrs. Turner said, an amused look in her beautiful large brown eyes. Kincaid's mother, Melissa Turner, was tall and slim like her daughter. Brown-black hair framed her pretty face.

After lunch Kincaid helped Nancy, Bess, and George saddle up for their ride out to see Lulu and Justice.

5

"Bess, you can have Miss Penny," Kincaid said, as Bess headed immediately for the stall of a beautiful copper-colored mare with a rippling mane. The horse whinnied as Bess approached.

"I think she remembers me from the last time I was here," Bess said, stroking the horse's head as she talked.

"Could be," Kincaid replied as she led out a large black horse with a jagged streak of white across its nose. "This is Flash," she said, smiling at George. "I think you'll like him."

While George saddled up, Kincaid took Nancy to where two Appaloosas waited impatiently. "You're ready for a run, aren't you, Misty?" Kincaid asked. One of the huge horses snorted and bobbed its large head as she neared.

"Nancy, you can have Paha Sapa," Kincaid said, handing Nancy the reins of the other Appaloosa. "*Paha Sapa* is the Sioux name for the Black Hills."

When everyone was finally ready, Kincaid led them out of the barn and up a trail that cut across the ranch.

It was a clear, sunny day, and Nancy felt as if she could see forever. At first they rode through flat pasture, but then the ground began to roll into the low hills of the Great Plains.

The horses stepped through green prairie grasses and bright-colored wildflowers. Shadows from the clouds threw patches of grayish purple across the ground. Occasionally a soft wind would kick up, strong enough to ruffle the horses' manes and swirl dust and tumbleweeds across the path.

"This is so beautiful," Bess said with a sigh. "I always love coming here."

"I can see why," Nancy said, smiling.

"I feel like cutting loose a little," Kincaid said. "Anybody else game?"

"I'm ready," George called, and the others nodded their agreement. Following Kincaid's lead, they guided their horses off the trail. Within minutes they were galloping across a field of buttercups at full speed.

When Kincaid finally pulled up Misty, the others followed her lead, bringing their panting horses to a stop.

"I knew Bess was good, but you two are excellent riders, too," Kincaid said to George and Nancy. "If I didn't know any better, I'd think you all grew up on a ranch or a farm." As she talked she led the others over to a small pond, where she reined her horse in to a stop.

"I don't ride as often as I'd like," Nancy said.

"That's because you're too busy solving crimes and working on cases," George said.

"Well, I sure hope you can help us," Kincaid said, climbing down from her horse. "We've got to stop this rustling, or we'll be bankrupt." She led her horse to the edge of the pond and dropped the reins, so he could drink.

Bess slid down and led Miss Penny to the pond.

7

The others followed her lead. While the horses drank and rested, Nancy and the others sat on a rocky outcropping and talked.

"Who might be rustling your family's herd?" Nancy asked Kincaid. "Do you have any suspects?"

"My dad is sure it's Badger Brady," Kincaid answered, making a face.

"From the look on your face, I take it he's not one of your favorite people," George said.

"He's not," Kincaid said. "He's Dad's chief competitor—has his own ranch near the Badlands. Dad thinks he's trying to drive us out of business. They've had some bad history together. They were in business together once—ten years ago, but it went bankrupt. Dad says it was Badger's fault. Dad's sure Badger stole money from the business, but he couldn't prove it. They had a huge fight and haven't spoken to each other since—except to yell when they run into each other."

"But if they've had this feud for that long, why would Badger start rustling now?" Nancy asked.

"This isn't the first thing he's tried," Kincaid said. She stood up and began pacing back and forth. Nancy could see that she was very upset. "He's been causing us trouble for years. He filed a libel suit against Dad for some of the things he believes Dad has said, paid one of our ranch hands to mess up our accounting books, and even started his own bison ranch as competition."

"But why does your dad think he's started rustling?" Nancy persisted.

"Dad heard Badger is having a really hard time financially lately," Kincaid said. "He's had to let go of most of his ranch hands. He even sold some of his breeding stock. It figures that it would be a lot easier for him if he could drive us out of business."

"Does your dad have any proof that Badger Brady might be behind the rustling?" Bess asked.

"Nope," Kincaid said with a sigh. "Nothing. Whoever it is, he—or she—hasn't left any clues so far." She walked over to Misty, who stood patiently waiting. Stroking the horse's thick neck, Kincaid said, "Well, what about it, old girl? You ready to go see Justice?"

The four climbed back in their saddles and continued the journey to the area where Kincaid had isolated Justice and his mother Lulu.

When they had ridden another fifteen minutes, they came to a hill of rock that had a distinctive flat top. The sides of the hill were covered in dark green brush and purple prairie clover. Kincaid pulled her horse around to face the others and said, "The corral and shelter are right around this mesa. Let's dismount and walk the rest of the way. I don't want to startle Lulu."

As they walked, leading their horses, Nancy watched Kincaid. For the first time that day, the worries of the world seemed to leave her friend.

"I can't wait until you see him," Kincaid said. "He's the cutest baby I've ever seen."

As they rounded the small hill, Nancy felt a

sudden stab of alarm as she looked at the scene before her. The corral gate was open. Beyond was a large heap of rubble—large chunks and slabs of wood were tangled with piles of grasses and hay.

"Oh no!" Kincaid cried. "They're gone! Justice and Lulu are gone!"

2

Rattled!

Kincaid ran through the open corral gate, followed closely by Nancy, Bess, and George. Quickly she began tearing through the splintered wood and scattered piles of feed.

"Be careful, Kincaid," Nancy warned. "Don't hurt yourself."

"This was the shelter," Kincaid said. Nancy could see tears starting to flood the young woman's eyes. "This pile of wood was Justice and Lulu's shelter."

They all looked at the mess. "It looks like it's been hacked by an axe," Bess murmured, shaking her head.

"This is terrible," Kincaid said. "This isn't like

the other rustlings. They didn't destroy stuff like this."

"Is it possible that this isn't related to the other rustlings?" Nancy asked gently. "Could this have been done by someone else?"

"What do you mean?" Kincaid said, her voice shaky, her eyes wide with shock.

"If the method is different, it could mean this was done by a different criminal," Nancy said, checking the ground.

"What are you looking for?" Kincaid asked.

"Anything that might tell us something about what happened here," Nancy murmured. "Do these look like they could be Lulu's and Justice's prints?"

Kincaid crouched to check out the spot where Nancy was pointing. "Yes," she said. "See? These would be Lulu's, and the little ones would be Justice's."

Nancy and the others followed the trail out of the corral for about thirty yards. Then the prints disappeared. "The wind has been pretty heavy off and on today," Nancy said. "Maybe it kicked the dust up and hid the tracks."

"Wait," Kincaid said. "We can check that out." She pulled up a clump of tall, stiff prairie grass and used it like a brush to remove the top layer of dirt. "I do this when I come across what might be a prehistoric dig site and I don't have any brushes with me. It works just fine."

The others watched her graze the tips of the

grass across the dirt. Slowly, the hoofprints came back into sight. "There," she said. "See? It worked."

"Wow," George said. "You have to be so careful not to brush away the prints themselves."

"Well, it helps that the dirt is so hard in this area. When it packs and dries, it's almost like clay."

She continued to brush the dirt away. Then they followed the trail of the two animals another twenty yards to where the prints seemed to turn, then back up, then stop once and for all.

"It's as though they disappeared," Bess said in a hushed voice.

"Or were hauled away," Kincaid said. "They'd have to use a special livestock trailer."

She continued brushing the dirt, and little by little, a set of tire tracks appeared—first two, then two farther ahead, then three fairly close together.

"We don't have all the tracks, but it looks like a large trailer, pulled by a sport utility vehicle or a four-by-four," Kincaid said. "The tracks seem to go off to the west. I'm going to ride out that way and see if I can find anything."

"I'll go with you," Bess said, climbing into her saddle. She seemed eager to start the chase.

"George and I will stay here," Nancy said. "I want to nose around a little more."

As she watched Bess and Kincaid ride off to follow the tire tracks, Nancy had an idea. "Come on, George, we have work to do," she said.

She walked to the shattered shelter and dug

13

through the debris until she found a pitchfork. "I thought I saw this sticking through the boards," she said.

"So what are we doing?" George asked.

"Well, Kincaid said the dirt in this area is almost like clay, right?"

"Right."

"Grab some shorter pieces of broken boards," Nancy said. "I want to try something."

While George picked out some boards, Nancy found a bucket and filled it from Lulu and Justice's water trough. Then she led George back to the tire tracks. Carefully, Nancy cleaned the tire tracks of as much extra dirt as she could with Kincaid's grass brush without wiping away the tracks themselves.

Then she and George took turns with the pitchfork digging up clumps of dirt from the ground a few yards away from the tracks. They piled the dirt into a mound; then Nancy pushed out a well in the center of the pile.

"What are we doing?" George asked.

"Making modeling clay," Nancy said. Slowly, she dribbled a little water from the bucket into the well in the center of the mound of dirt. Little by little, she pulled dirt from the edge of the pile into the well of water in the center. As the dirt absorbed the water, it became gooey.

"Looks like we're making mud to me," George said, shaking her head.

"Exactly," Nancy agreed. "Mud pies."

Carefully, she added more water, then more dirt,

then repeated both steps until she had the consistency she wanted. It was no longer gooey; it held together like clay. When she pressed the palm of her hand into it, it made a perfect print. "Hand me a board," she said.

George handed Nancy one of the short pieces of board from the shelter. Nancy smeared some of the clay she had made onto the board, then placed it, clay side down, on one of the tire tracks. "We have to push very gently," she said, pressing carefully with just a few fingers. "We want to get the print, but we don't want to smear it, and we don't want the clay to fall off."

It took a few attempts, but she finally got the technique right—just the right amount of mud-clay on the board, just the right amount of pressure against the tire track. By that time, the track she had been working on was too smeared to be of any use, but she and George imprinted the other tracks.

When they were finished, they had four boards imprinted with tire tracks and laid out, clay side up, in the sun to dry. George gazed into the distance, shielding her eyes from the light. "I think I see Bess and Kincaid returning," she said.

"Let's look around a little more until they get here," Nancy said, leading George back into the corral.

When Kincaid and Bess arrived, they were tired and discouraged. "We found nothing," Bess said, slipping down off Miss Penny. "The trail just petered out."

"It looks like they went over the grass at one point," Kincaid said, "and we couldn't pick up the trail after that."

Nancy and George showed them the models they had made of the tire tracks, and Bess's and Kincaid's spirits seemed to lift a little.

"We were just looking around to see if we could find any more clues," George said.

"We'll help," Bess said as she and Kincaid joined the search. Occasionally, one of them would find something, but none of the items seemed significant. Bess found a hammer, but Kincaid recognized it as one of her dad's. They came across some rusty barbed wire, shotgun shells, and a coil of rope, but Kincaid had explanations for all of them.

"Hey, what's this?" George called out. She held up a curved gray-white object, about eleven inches long.

The other three rushed over. "Oh, that's a tooth," Kincaid said casually. "Probably from a saber-toothed tiger. Keep it." She turned and walked back to where she had been searching.

"A saber-toothed tiger!" George said, turning the object over in her hand. "Cool."

"Sure," Kincaid called back. "We find stuff like that all the time. This whole area is crawling with prehistoric remnants. People come from all over the world to set up digs around here. Here's some petrified wood."

She reached down and picked up two pieces of what looked like rectangles of red-brown stone.

16

The surfaces looked as if someone had run a comb over them, etching tiny lines in the rock.

"This is why I call it one of my secret places. This is almost at the center of our ranch. There's no road here. Part of the area is concealed by the hill. I have several places like this scattered around where I've done some archaeological digs. It should have been a very safe place for Lulu and Justice."

She gave the pieces of petrified wood to Nancy, then said, "I know that looking for clues is important, but I've got to tell my parents what happened. I'm going back."

Nancy could hear the distress in Kincaid's voice. She was sure the initial shock was wearing off. The full impact of what had happened was beginning to register with her new friend.

As she turned to leave the area, Nancy noticed something shining in the grass. "Look," she said. "This may be something." She leaned over to look closer. As the others gathered around her, Nancy untied the bandanna from around her neck and used it as a glove to pick up a big, rusty metal disc.

"Looks like a hubcap," George said.

"Yeah, but a weird one," Bess said, squinting in the sunlight. "What's that mark in the middle?"

They all looked closer. It was an old hubcap, dented and pockmarked with rust. "It looks like some kind of design," Nancy said, looking at the rusty scratches across the center. "Could it be the brand of one of the ranches?"

Kincaid leaned in to look closer. "I don't recognize it," she said. "But it's so messed up, I can't really see what it is exactly."

"But it's not familiar to you, right?" Nancy asked. "It wouldn't be from one of the vehicles on your ranch?"

"No," Kincaid said, shaking her head.

"Maybe it's from the vehicle that took Lulu and Justice away," Bess said. "Nancy, that's a real clue. Kincaid, I'm sure we're going to find Lulu and her calf."

"Oh, Bess, I hope you're right," Kincaid said. "I'm going back. Do you still want to look around? I can send someone to lead you home."

"No, I'm ready to go," Nancy said. Carefully, she picked up the hubcap with her bandanna and gently slipped it into her saddlebag.

The others mounted their horses, and Nancy handed each of them a board with the tire track impression. Kincaid, George, and Bess carefully held the short boards in front of them. Nancy placed the board she would carry on a pile of rubble from the destroyed shelter. Then she climbed on Paha Sapa and walked him over to the pile so she could pick up her board.

She started to reach for the board to hold it over her horse's back for the journey home. As she leaned over, Paha Sapa became a little jittery. He backed up, turned, then moved forward again. A whinny of protest rippled his lips.

"Easy, boy," Nancy cooed to the Appaloosa. "Just let me get this board and we'll start on

18

home." Paha Sapa would go only so far forward, and when Nancy urged him on, he resisted.

"What's happening?" George called.

"My horse won't get near that pile of rubble," Nancy said. "I'm trying to grab the last board."

"Here," Kincaid said, riding over. "I'll get it and hand it to you."

They both heard the sound at the same time. It started soft and slow, then grew loud and very fast. Nancy saw the snake first, almost camouflaged in the wreckage. It was a thick, mottled coil with a tapering head in the center. At the end of its tail, a small brown rattle shook with menace.

"Kincaid! Do you see it?" Nancy whispered.

"No, but I sure can hear it," Kincaid said. She reined in her horse. "There it is. I see it."

Nancy could feel Paha Sapa's heart beating as she tried to calm him. Her own heart was pounding just as fast.

Suddenly—as if it were on a spring—the snake shot forward.

3

A Chilling Call

Paha Sapa reared up, and Nancy slipped down on the saddle. She threw her arms around the horse's huge neck and clung there.

"Nancy!" Kincaid said. "Hold on. I'll take care of the snake." She reached for the pitchfork and rode to where Nancy was desperately trying to stay on her horse.

Paha Sapa was still reared up, dancing on his rear hooves, trying to dodge the poisonous fangs of the rattler. The snake sidled this way and that, aiming for the legs of Nancy's horse.

Nancy's arms were still wrapped tightly around Paha Sapa's thick neck, her fingers holding the reins so tightly they were numb. She was hanging almost vertically, her legs dangling out of the stirrups.

At last Kincaid and her horse, Misty, reached Nancy. With one experienced swoop, Kincaid thunked the pitchfork into the rattlesnake, directly behind its head. Its tail thrashed for a moment. Then it was still.

"Easy, boy, easy," Kincaid cooed to Paha Sapa. At last the great horse lowered its front legs back to earth. Nancy, her hands still grasping the reins and the horse's neck, plopped back onto the saddle.

"Thank you," Nancy said, smiling at Kincaid. "I sure understand the term *horsepower* now."

Kincaid picked up the last board with the clay tire tracks and handed it to Nancy. Nancy placed it gently over Paha Sapa's back. She held the board tightly with one hand and gave her horse several grateful pats with the other.

At last, carefully holding the boards across their horses' shoulders, the four friends headed toward the open pasture. They followed Kincaid along the trail back to the ranch compound. After they put their horses into their stalls, they carried the tire impressions up to the ranch house. Nancy also carried the hubcap, which she had dropped in a burlap bag she had found in the stable.

Melissa stepped off the back porch to greet them. "What on earth are those?" she asked as the girls arranged the tire track models on the grass.

"This is terrible," Melissa Turner said when her daughter told her what she and the others had discovered. "Lulu and Justice. Kincaid, honey, I'm so sorry. I know you feel awful, but don't worry. We'll get them back, I'm sure. Your dad's in town picking up some feed. I'll call him."

Nancy saw the sadness in Mrs. Turner's eyes. She's not that sure, Nancy thought. She's trying to cheer up Kincaid, but she's worried that they'll never see Lulu and Justice again.

Nancy and the others followed Mrs. Turner into the kitchen to call Kincaid's father. Then she called the sheriff. "They'll both be here as soon as they can," she said when she finally hung up the phone. "Your dad's real upset," she reported to Kincaid, putting an arm around her daughter's shoulders.

Mrs. Turner sighed, peered out the kitchen window and then back at her daughter. Nancy could see that Kincaid's mother was also very upset. The broad welcoming smile she had greeted them with had changed—her lips were now set in a tight straight line. Nancy was sure she was fighting back tears, too.

"You go get cleaned up," Mrs. Turner finally said. "I'm going to start dinner. By the time we get through talking to the sheriff, it'll be time to eat." She took a deep breath.

George followed Kincaid and Mrs. Turner into the huge kitchen to help with dinner before freshening up.

Nancy and Bess headed toward their cabin, Nancy carrying the burlap bag with the hubcap in it.

When they arrived, she slipped the hubcap out of the bag and onto a small table by the window.

"What are you doing?" Bess asked, looking at the odd scratches in the middle of the hubcap.

"I'm going to make a pencil rubbing," Nancy said. "Maybe then we can see the design better."

"Nancy, what did you mean when you said that Lulu and Justice might have been taken by a different criminal?" Bess asked. "Are you saying this might not have been just a rustling? That maybe by tearing their shelter up, someone was trying to give the Turners some kind of warning?"

"It could be," Nancy said. She took a blank piece of paper and placed it over the center of the hubcap, where the rusty scratches were.

"Or do you mean that maybe it wasn't a regular rustling?" Bess suggested. "Maybe someone was specifically after Lulu and Justice?"

"That's possible, too," Nancy said. She took a soft pencil and lightly rubbed across the paper.

Slowly, a picture began to form on the paper. It was like a photographic negative—dark with faint white markings in the middle.

"It sort of looks like a flower," Bess said. "But not exactly. What is it, Nancy?"

"I'm not sure," Nancy said, standing up. "Well, let's get washed up and back to the house. The sheriff will be here shortly and I want to make sure he gets the hubcap and this rubbing."

Nancy and Bess returned to the ranch house just

as Bill Turner strode in. He was tall and handsome, with brown wavy hair. He looked very angry, but when he gave Kincaid a lopsided grin, his whole expression changed. "Don't you worry, honey," he said. "We'll get that buzzard once and for all, and Lulu and Justice will be back before you know it."

Kincaid hugged her father, burying her tear-streaked face into his shoulder. Nancy watched as Kincaid's parents flashed worried glances at each other over Kincaid's head.

Then Mr. Turner focused on Nancy. His dark blue eyes squinted as he stared at her intently. "Missy tells me you're quite a detective," he said, nodding toward Melissa Turner. "Let's see what you brought back."

As the girls showed Kincaid's father the tire track impressions, Nancy heard the sheriff's truck pull to a stop outside the ranch house.

"Hi, Bill . . . Melissa," the sheriff said, tipping his wide-brimmed hat. "What's been happening here? More bison gone, hmmm?" He reminded Nancy of a football player with his thick, muscular body and close-cropped blond hair. Nancy figured he was probably about the same age as Kincaid's parents.

"Matt, this has got to be stopped," Mr. Turner yelled. "This time it was two of my daughter's— the one from the fair and her calf. They were isolated from the rest of the herd so that Kincaid could raise the little one and groom it for the 4-H circuit. Had a pen and shelter for them out by

Cloud Mesa. Now they're gone, the shelter's destroyed, and my daughter's heart is broken. What are you going to do about it?"

"Calm down, Bill," the sheriff said. "It's not going to do any good to yell at me. I'm not going to find the culprits any faster that way."

"These are friends of Kincaid," Melissa Turner said. She gently put a hand on her husband's arm while she introduced Nancy, Bess, and George. "Girls, this is Sheriff Matt Switzer. He's an old friend of ours and a real good lawman. Tell him what you found."

Nancy told the sheriff about the site and then showed him the clay tire track models dried on the pieces of board.

"Well, now," Sheriff Switzer said. "Looks like we have some amateur detectives helping us."

"Nancy is not exactly an amateur," Bess said, proudly. "She has solved many crimes and has been a big help to law enforcement officials all over the country."

"And beyond," George added. "Show him what else we found, Nancy."

Nancy unwrapped the hubcap and offered it to the sheriff.

"So, what do we have here?" he asked, leaning in to check it out more closely. "A hubcap, hmmmm?"

Nancy told him where she had found it and showed him her pencil rubbing of it.

"Doesn't really look like much of anything, does

it?" he said, squinting at the smeary picture. "It's pretty rusty. It could have been up there for ages and could be anybody's."

The sheriff dropped the hubcap back in the bag. "But I'll take it along with me, just in case. These tire tracks, now," he said, peering closely at the models Nancy and George had made. "These are something else. They're real clear. Could be a big help. Thanks, you two. This is good work." He smiled at Nancy and George.

"Look, Matt," Mr. Turner said. "Do you have any clues? This makes over ten percent of our herd rustled now, and we don't seem to be any closer to getting it stopped. Have you checked out Badger Brady again?"

"I told you before, we've decided it's being done by outsiders," the sheriff replied. "There's a gang been coming down from Canada and rustling cattle and horses from upper Minnesota and North Dakota. Seems reasonable they could be coming farther south and picking off your herd, too."

"Well, let's get whoever's doing this," Mr. Turner said. "I want someone to pay for this." His dark brown eyes flashed with anger.

"We're working on it, we're working on it," the sheriff said. "But it's not that simple. They're pretty slippery. 'Bout the time we get close, they've hopped back across the border."

Nancy could see Mr. Turner's lips tighten in fury and frustration.

"I know it's hard to be patient, Bill," the sheriff

said. "But we're going to get them. We've got the law in three states working on this—and even the Royal Canadian Mounted Police are helping us out." Nancy felt a chill as a cool breeze kicked up the dust in the drive.

He turned to Kincaid. "Don't worry, little lady," he said. "With the Canadian Mounties helping us, we're bound to get your calf back." He smiled at Nancy and the others and nodded at the cloth-wrapped hubcap in his hand. "And with you three working on the case, too, we can't fail." He got into his pickup and backed around, then waved as he took off down the drive.

"He's so calm about this, he makes me crazy," Mr. Turner said, his hands clenched into tight fists.

"I know, honey," Mrs. Turner said. "But you and Matt have been friends since grade school. You know how he is. He's slow and methodical. Likes to get everything in place before he acts. Not like you," she added with a small smile.

"Dad's a man of action," Kincaid told her friends. Nancy recognized the pride in the young woman's voice.

"Oh, goodness—my pies!" Mrs. Turner suddenly yelled. She ran toward the house, followed closely by Kincaid and Bess.

"I'm going to do some chores," Mr. Turner said, his long legs striding toward the barn. "When's dinner?"

"Half an hour," Mrs. Turner called as she disappeared into the kitchen.

27

"You two want to help?" Mr. Turner called back to Nancy and George.

"Love to," George said, following him.

"I'll be right there," Nancy said. "I want to get a drink of water." She walked into the ranch house just as the phone rang. She could hear laughter from the kitchen as Mrs. Turner, Kincaid, and Bess appeared to be rescuing the pies.

The phone rang again, and Kincaid yelled from the kitchen with a shriek of laughter. "Someone get that. Our hands are full."

Nancy walked to the old-fashioned phone table in the hallway and picked up the receiver.

"Hello," she said. "This is the M-Bar-B—"

"I know who it is," hissed the low voice through the receiver. "I was hoping you'd answer."

Nancy's heart pounded, and the hairs on the back of her neck stood at attention. The voice sounded as if it were from another world—eerie and hushed.

"Don't try to find your little calf or you'll be very sorry," the caller continued. "I'm only going to warn you once."

4

The Jawbone Talks

Nancy shuddered as a chill rippled across her shoulders. This time it was not caused by the South Dakota breeze. The threatening words of the anonymous phone call still echoed in her mind—even after the caller had hung up and she walked into the kitchen.

"Nancy?" Bess's cheery voice interrupted Nancy's thoughts. "What's the matter?"

Nancy told Bess, Kincaid, and Mrs. Turner about the phone call. "He must have thought I was you, Kincaid. It was hard to tell because the voice was so low and whispery, but the person may have an accent."

"What kind of accent?" Kincaid asked.

"I'm not sure," Nancy said, going over the words

in her head. "A sort of jumbled German, maybe. Or he might have been trying to disguise his voice and made it sound strange."

"Oh my," Melissa Turner said. "What a horrible thing to do—call and scare us like that. This has to stop. I am not going to allow my family to be bullied any longer! We've got to get to the bottom of this."

"You're right, Mom," Kincaid said, slamming a spoon back into a pot of chili on the countertop. Drops of reddish brown sauce sizzled on the pale green tile. "I'm tired of being robbed and threatened."

Kincaid yanked off the apron she had loosely tied around her waist and threw it onto a chair. "Mom, you call Matt and tell him about the call," she said. "Bess, you and I will go to the barn to tell Dad. Then we're going to eat. An army needs food to fight a war." She stormed out of the kitchen, and Bess ran out the door after her.

Over dinner Nancy, Bess, George, and the Turners talked about the rustling.

"Matt said he'd put a tracer on our phone in case we get another call," Mr. Turner said.

As Nancy buttered a large chunk of Melissa Turner's homemade corn bread, she felt another shudder at the memory of that low, eerie voice.

"What proof do you have that Badger Brady might be the rustler, Mr. Turner?" Nancy asked.

"He's the logical suspect," Mr. Turner replied, his lips tightly drawn in a narrow smile.

Nancy could tell he really didn't want to talk about Badger Brady with his visitors, so she decided to drop the subject.

No one spoke for a few minutes, each lost in thought. Finally George broke the silence. "What about that hubcap?" she asked. "Don't you think that could be a clue?"

"Matt says it's so old and rusty, it could have been up there for ages," Mrs. Turner said. "Or, it could have been lost by somebody driving around there, not necessarily the rustlers."

"But I don't understand," George said. "How could someone just drive out there to the shelter? Your ranch is fenced, right?"

"Sure, but it's a thousand acres," Mr. Turner said. "We can't monitor the entire perimeter all the time. We make regular fence and barbed-wire checks, but there's not someone watching every yard of fence every day."

"And a lot of stuff can disturb a ranch fence," Melissa Turner added. "A charging animal, a high prairie wind—"

"A pair of wire cutters," Kincaid grumbled.

"Once a fence is breached, an intruder has pretty much free rein," Mr. Turner said. "There are no roads, so you need a pretty good vehicle."

"But everybody out here has one of those," Mrs. Turner pointed out.

"But *just anybody* still shouldn't be driving around there, Mom," Kincaid said. "That's our property."

"Yes, but people do wander off the road sometimes and get lost," Mrs. Turner said. "When there are no road markers or houses or anything—nothing but miles and miles of open land—it's hard to find your way back to civilization."

After dinner Nancy, Bess, and George helped Kincaid clean up; then all four went to the guest cabin to talk.

George put the petrified wood fragments and the prehistoric tiger tooth on the windowsill. "These are so cool," she said. She held up the tooth, turning it so it shimmered in the moonlight. "Did you say you find a lot of this stuff around here?"

"Mmm-hmm," Kincaid answered. "This whole area attracts archaeologists and paleontologists from all over the world."

"Tell them about your national science project," Bess urged. "Go on—don't be modest."

"Well," Kincaid said, "I worked at the geology museum as a summer intern. I'd found a baby mammoth jawbone on the west end of the ranch."

"You're kidding!" George said.

"Nope. I studied it to determine what it ate. You can tell a lot about the diet of a fossilized jawbone by the shape the teeth are in."

"Got her to the national finals," Bess said proudly.

"Very cool," George said, studying the tooth.

Kincaid turned on the small television set. "It's almost time for the local news," she said. "I want to see if they mention the rustling."

They watched for half an hour, but there was nothing said about Lulu and Justice.

"I should have known," Kincaid said as the weather forecaster began predicting a beautiful day for tomorrow. "What's the big deal about a couple of missing bison, right?"

"Maybe it's intentional," Bess said. "Maybe it is those guys from Canada who did it. Maybe the two countries are setting up a sting to catch them. If that's the case, the less said on the news about any of it, the better."

"There's one part that bothers me, though," Nancy said.

"What?" George asked, putting the tooth back on the windowsill and rejoining the group around the fireplace.

"If we're dealing with an international ring of rustlers, why did they take Lulu and Justice?" Nancy pointed out. "How did they even know they were out there? Why not just keep on taking a few at a time from the main herd? And why make that threatening call? If these guys are two-country rustling professionals, I don't think they'd be phoning the victims personally."

"Come to think of it," Bess said, "you're right. The caller said 'your little calf.' How did the person know Lulu and Justice were Kincaid's?"

"Hey," George said. "Are you saying you don't think this Canadian gang stole those two?"

"I don't know what I'm saying exactly," Nancy said. "It just doesn't seem to add up. The caller seemed to know who Kincaid was—or at least knew *about* her, and that Lulu and Justice were hers."

"Someone who knows me . . ." Kincaid murmured.

"Or at least knows *about* you," Nancy repeated.

"You mean someone local," Bess said. "You mean Badger Brady."

"Maybe," Nancy said. "Kincaid, tell me more about him. What's his real name?"

"He grew up around here," Kincaid began. "Went to school with my dad and Matt as I told you. Dad always said he was called Badger because badgers have such nasty temperaments and they're such vicious animals when cornered."

"If he's so dangerous," Nancy asked, "why did your dad go into business with him?"

"Badger wasn't always so bad," Kincaid continued. "His dad and uncle went to prison for cheating on their taxes and not paying their bills, and the whole family's been in trouble off and on forever. Badger got into some scrapes when he was younger, but he seemed to straighten up. Dad figured starting a ranch together might give Badger the chance he needed to turn out better than the rest of his family."

"After he and your dad broke up their business," George said, "how did he start his own buffalo ranch?"

"He left the area for a few years," Kincaid

answered. She stretched her legs, then draped them over the wooden arm of the worn leather chair. "Then back he came, flashing a lot of money and buying up bison stock from Colorado. The next thing we knew, he had a herd big enough to give Dad some real competition. And then he was back to his old ways."

"What do you mean?" Nancy asked.

"Well, we heard rumors that some of his stock was sick but he sells them as if they're healthy," Kincaid said.

"That's pretty unethical," Bess said.

"He falsifies records, swindles customers, and cheats on his federal inspections," George said. "And now he's maybe a rustler to boot."

"Do you think the sheriff suspects him at all? I know he thinks a Canadian gang did it," Nancy said to Kincaid.

"Matt knows Badger from school," Kincaid answered. "He agrees he could be a suspect, and has even checked out Badger's ranch. But there's no sign of any of our missing herd there—or anywhere. And you heard Matt. He seems to be leaning toward the gang from Canada."

"Do you brand the bison?" Nancy asked.

"Sort of," Kincaid answered. "We tattoo the inside of one ear."

"The phone call might be a beginning," Nancy said. "I'd like to hear Badger Brady's voice— especially over the phone. Maybe we can work up a

35

sting of our own." In the background, the sports reporter finished up his story, and the station broke for a commercial.

Kincaid reached over to turn up the set. "They always end the news show with a short feature about something local," she said. "It's their last chance to mention Lulu and Justice."

As they watched, the program returned to the news desk. "And now for our final story," the anchorwoman said. "Local personality Antoinette Francoeur has made the headlines again. You might recall that last year, she released all the parakeets and cockatiels from a pet shop."

"Why would she do that?" Bess asked.

"She said she doesn't believe in confining animals for any reason," Kincaid said.

"Francoeur has scheduled a press conference for tomorrow morning at ten at Beauforêt, her estate in the Black Hills," the anchorwoman continued. "She is expected to announce the formation of a new organization dedicated to liberating all animals."

"What happened to her last year after the pet shop incident?" Nancy asked.

"She paid a fine, but that's all," Kincaid answered. "And she can afford it. You should see her place. My dad pointed it out to me once when we were driving in the mountains."

"More important, what happened to all the rabbits and birds she set free?" Bess wondered.

"Some were recaptured and returned to the pet shop," Kincaid said. "But others were never found.

Someone saw a couple of parakeets flying around the park a couple of weeks ago, as a matter of fact, but they couldn't catch them."

"Does she think *all* animals should be set free?" George asked.

"I guess so," Kincaid said with a shrug.

"Hey," Bess said, jumping up from her chair. "What about buffalo on a ranch?"

"You mean that she might have . . . Oh, Bess!" Kincaid exclaimed, her eyes wide. "What if Antoinette Francoeur stole Lulu and Justice?"

"But she wouldn't steal them," Nancy pointed out. "Isn't it her idea to let them run free?"

"Who knows exactly?" Kincaid said. "A lot of people think she's not really an activist—she's just a nut. There have been a lot of rumors about her past. Somebody said she got in trouble the last place she lived because she released horses from riding academies. Then I heard she was letting guard dogs loose and breaking monkeys out of their cages at a zoo somewhere."

"That doesn't sound like someone who really cares about animals," Nancy said. "Some animals couldn't survive in the wild after they'd been taken care of all their lives."

"Sounds like she doesn't care much for humans, either," Bess said, making a face. "I wouldn't be too thrilled to be living somewhere with a lot of guard dogs running around loose."

"Those are just rumors," Kincaid reminded them. "I know the pet shop stuff happened, but I'm not sure about the rest. But I do know Lulu. If that woman let her go, Lulu would lead Justice back to the herd. That's one of the reasons I separated them. I wanted to be able to raise Justice myself and train and groom him for the fairs."

"Maybe Antoinette learned a lesson from the pet shop incident," George offered. "Suppose she decided it would be better to kidnap animals and release them in a totally different area. That way, there would be less chance they'd be recaptured and returned. If all those stories are true, she sounds a little weird. Who knows what she might do."

"But would she hack the shelter to pieces?" Nancy wondered. "And make threatening calls?"

"You know, she might," Kincaid said. "I saw her on TV last year when she was being arrested. She was like a wild animal herself—kicking and yelling. It's amazing she didn't get jail time."

"Maybe we should see what she has to say at this press conference tomorrow," Nancy said. "I also want to check out Badger Brady."

"Sounds like it's going to be a busy day," George said. "Good! I'm ready for some action."

"Then let's do something fun tonight," Bess said. "Maybe go to the Stomp. Do they still have that great band there?"

"Yep," Kincaid said. "That's a good idea. I could use a little noisy music."

The Stomp was a young-adults club in a small strip mall perched on the edge of a mountain overlooking Rapid City, about ten miles from the Turners' ranch. A seven-piece band filled the wood-and-glass building with music, from country-western to reggae.

When they walked in, Kincaid spotted some friends in a booth and led the others over to them.

Kincaid led them to the table. "Hi, guys, you remember Bess from last summer. This is her cousin George and her friend Nancy. Girls, this is Angie, Clayton, and Gregg."

"Great to see you back, Bess," Angie said. "Hi, Nancy and George. Welcome." Angie had dark wavy hair and a friendly smile. Nancy smiled back.

A cute, brown-haired young man stood to let the girls slide into the booth. "Hi, I'm Clayton," he said. "Bess, I knew you'd be back."

Within a half hour more of Kincaid's friends joined them. They pushed several tables together and spent the next couple of hours hanging out, ordering sodas and fries, and dancing.

Finally Nancy suggested breaking it up. "We have a lot to do tomorrow," she reminded them.

"Yeah," Kincaid agreed. "That's fine with me." Suddenly she gasped. She stared over Nancy's shoulder. Her next words shot out like little darts between her clenched teeth: "It's him, Nancy. Badger Brady. Walking past the window."

"George, you and Bess pay the bill," Nancy said. "We'll meet you at the car."

Nancy and Kincaid raced out the door. Brady was halfway down the block. He was not very tall,

39

but his body was stocky, so he seemed big. He walked with a long stride, and Nancy and Kincaid had to hurry to keep up with him.

When Brady reached the end of the strip of shops, he paused for a moment. Nancy and Kincaid stepped behind some shrubs that bordered a fountain. After a few moments, Nancy peeked around the green branches. There was no one in sight.

"Come on," Nancy whispered. "He must have turned the corner." She and Kincaid stepped back onto the walkway.

"Just a minute," a brusque voice thundered. "Don't take another step."

5

A Reflection of Danger

In the glaring wash of the shop lights, Badger Brady's face was dark red and twisted with anger as he stepped from around the corner to face Nancy and Kincaid.

"What are you two doing, chasing after me?" he demanded. "Kincaid, you're just like your father. Always after me. Well, I'm going to put an end to it, do you hear me?"

"We're not afraid of you," Kincaid said in a low voice. Nancy put a hand on her friend's arm.

Brady's eyes narrowed as he looked at Nancy. She listened closely to his voice. Was he the one who made the threatening phone call? she wondered.

41

"We'll just see about that," Brady said. "You tell your father you saw me. You tell him what I said. The trouble between us is not over."

Brady glared at them for a few moments. People wandered onto the walkway from the shops. Brady glanced at them, then back at Nancy and Kincaid. With one final menacing glance, he bolted away.

Nancy and Kincaid retraced their steps to the Stomp parking lot, where Bess and George were waiting.

During the drive back to the ranch, Nancy related the encounter she and Kincaid had experienced.

"Sounds like Badger *is* a good name for that guy," George said.

Tuesday morning, over breakfast in the Turner kitchen, the girls made plans to attend Antoinette Francoeur's press conference that morning.

"Here, Nancy," Kincaid said. "You and I can wear these." She took out two official-looking press badges. "These are from my high school. I was the editor of the school newspaper."

Nancy changed a few letters so they read *RHI*. "We are now members of the press corps for the *River Heights Independent*," she said, and handed one of the badges to Kincaid before pinning a duplicate on her own blue blazer.

"Is that your hometown newspaper?" Kincaid asked, pinning her badge on her jeans jacket.

"Made it up," Nancy said, grinning. "Bess, you

have a camera. Kincaid, do you have one George can borrow? They can be press photographers."

"Let me at your computer, Kincaid," Bess said. Within minutes Bess's computer design talent paid off, and she had created two impressive press photographer passes.

"All right," Nancy said. "Off to the press conference."

Kincaid drove them into the Black Hills in her heavy-duty, all-terrain vehicle. "You're not going to believe it up here," Bess told Nancy and George. "Wait until you see the houses. We're not talking mountain cabins, folks."

"I didn't know what to expect when we were talking about coming here," George said. "First of all, I thought the Black Hills *were* hills. I didn't realize they were mountains."

"It's one of the oldest mountain ranges in the world," Bess said. "Older than the Alps or the Himalayas."

"And it's the highest range in the U.S. east of the Rockies," Kincaid said proudly. "The Black Hills cover an area the same size as Delaware."

"There—look at that," Bess said, pointing out the window. "Would you believe you'd see a house like that in the middle of a mountain forest?"

Nancy and George followed Bess's gaze over to a huge mansion. It was built in the southern style—redbrick, with two-story white columns and long verandas on both floors filled with wicker furniture.

"Whoa—how about that one," George said as they drove up the road. An enormous glass-and-steel flat-roofed house jutted out over the side of the mountain cliff. It was supported from below by diagonal steel beams.

As they climbed farther, they saw more incredible homes. Some were in the open, showy and extravagant. Others they had to squint to see because they were set back from the road. Shielded behind a curtain of dense dark green pine and spruce trees, they seemed to be purposely hidden.

"I expected log cabins and maybe a few chalets," Nancy said. "Nothing like this."

Kincaid drove around two more winding curves, then slowed the car. "Here we are," she said. Two guards stopped the vehicle as she pulled up to a gate. The girls showed their badges and passes, and the guards motioned them through.

After another short winding climb, they came to a small parking area, where they were waved into a parking place. Then the four joined the group of about fifty media people climbing the steps from the parking lot to Beauforêt, Antoinette Francoeur's mansion.

"*Beauforêt*," Nancy murmured. "That means 'beautiful woods.' Well, she sure has that right." Nancy looked ahead to a huge house. It had eight sides and was constructed of wood and glass.

The front of the house hung out over the valley, supported by huge log braces that angled back into the cliff.

Ushers guided the crowd around the house to the rear terrace from which they had a marvelous view of the surrounding mountains and canyons. Nancy noticed several other buildings on the estate— barns, stable, smaller houses. Could one of them hold a buffalo cow and her calf? she wondered.

Her thoughts were interrupted by a flutter of commotion as the huge double doors opened onto the terrace. Through the doors swooped a strikingly tall woman, at least six feet tall, with a long neck and long arms. "How old is she?" Nancy whispered to Kincaid.

"I read once that she was in her fifties," Kincaid whispered back.

"Welcome to Beauforêt," Antoinette Francoeur said with a slight accent. "I am pleased you have joined us this morning," she added, shaking her thick mane of long silvery blond hair, which fell down her back. She wore a gauzy purple dress, with a long full skirt. The only jewelry she wore were lacy gold earrings that hung to her shoulders.

Nancy felt a gentle poke in her ribs from Bess. "Did you catch her feet?" Bess said. Nancy moved so she could peer through the crowd to see the woman's feet. They were bare. An elastic bandage was wrapped around her right ankle.

"This is a grand moment for me," the unusually dressed Frenchwoman continued. "I am happy to announce the creation of Justice for Animals." Nancy heard Kincaid gasp behind her.

"I doubt that it means anything," Nancy whispered. "Justice for Animals is a logical name for an animal protection group. It probably doesn't have anything to do with your calf."

Ms. Francoeur continued her prepared statement about the organization and how she wanted to form a coalition with other groups so she could set up an international network.

"This will be my finest deed, to establish and provide financial backing for this organization," the woman said. "We will search out and find animals that need our help—and then do what we need to do. I hope you all will stay to view a short video that has been prepared for your enlightenment. After that you are invited to a light buffet where we may talk more informally about Justice for Animals."

"Ms. Francoeur, is it true you believe all animals should live free and none should be contained for any reason?" asked one reporter.

"That is basically my desire, yes," the Frenchwoman replied.

"And is it true that you released gibbons from a zoo in Colorado?" another woman asked.

"I have never done anything so foolish," Ms. Francoeur said. "Such an animal could probably not survive on its own. I would like to see them out of zoos, of course. But first I would find a better place for them to be."

"What about buffalo?" Kincaid called out.

"Interesting that you should mention them," Antoinette Francoeur said. "We use two beautiful

South Dakota bison in our logo." She held up a poster for Justice for Animals. The logo included an artist's watercolor of a female bison and a calf grazing, with the Black Hills in the background.

Nancy heard Kincaid gasp again. "How do you feel about ranching bison?" Nancy asked, stepping forward. "About breeding them in captivity?"

"Enough questions for now," Ms. Francoeur said with a flip of her long fingers. "Let us go to my theater and watch the video. Then we will have a lovely buffet and talk some more."

She turned and sailed back through the large doorway. Slowly, the crowd filed in behind her.

As the others moved forward, Nancy began backing up. "Come on," she said, "this way." She moved quickly, followed by Bess, George, and Kincaid. Nancy never took her eyes off the guards standing by the doorway. No one saw her or the others as they separated from the crowd.

"We're not going to watch the movie, I take it," George said as the four eased behind two large blue spruce trees.

"I think I'd rather look around the grounds," Nancy said.

"Won't they miss us?" Bess asked. "After all, you and Kincaid asked questions."

"Probably not," Nancy explained. "I saw people pick up press kits from the table, then walk to the parking lot. Apparently, they weren't staying for the video and buffet. As far as anyone knows, we could have done the same."

They stayed behind the trees until they saw the two guards go inside the house.

"Now be quiet and be careful," Nancy warned the others. "There might be other guards or employees wandering around the grounds."

"Nancy . . . that poster," Kincaid said. "It looks just like Lulu and Justice. And the name for the group—Justice."

"I know it seems odd," Nancy said. "But it's probably just a coincidence."

"I agree," George said softly. "Justice for Animals is a pretty logical name, Kincaid."

"But the poster," Kincaid protested. "I could only see it from a distance, but it looks so much like Lulu and Justice. What if *Antoinette* took them?"

"You mean to let them run free?" Bess asked.

"Maybe," Kincaid said. "Or maybe she's going to use them as mascots. As symbols of majestic animals that shouldn't be in a pen."

"But she couldn't show them anywhere," George said. "If she did, your family or friends would recognize them—and she'd be busted."

"She couldn't show them around here," Kincaid agreed. "But she's setting up an international network. What better animal to take around the world as a symbol than the American bison? People in other countries have never even seen one. Lulu's so tame. She wouldn't give anybody any trouble. And Justice will go anywhere Lulu goes." Her voice was low as she looked away.

Then she turned back to Nancy, her voice sound-

48

ing frantic. "I'll bet she took them. They're probably here on the estate, waiting to be shipped to Europe for some Justice for Animals fund-raiser."

"Oh, Nancy, what if she's right," Bess said, her eyes wide with concern for her friend.

"Stay cool," Nancy warned. "We'll never find them if we take dumb chances. Everybody take a deep breath and calm down." She waited, then said, "Okay, let's look in that barn over there."

Nancy darted quickly from the house to a huge barn, always staying low and behind a clipped hedge or flowers for cover. One by one, the others followed. When they reached the barn, they circled around to the back. "We might attract attention if we open the front door," Nancy explained. "Let's see if there's another way in."

She finally found a service door at the rear of the building, but it was locked. She dug her lock pick from her purse and, within seconds, the door opened with a creepy creak.

"This doesn't smell like a barn," Bess said, closing the door. It made the same creaking whine.

The light was dim, but it got brighter as they moved to the front of the building. There, the large windows let in the sun, which bounced off dozens of shiny vehicles.

"Wow," George said in a soft voice, peeking into a pale blue sports car.

"It's filled with cars," Kincaid moaned. "The place is full of antique automobiles."

Lined up in perfect rows were Dusenbergs,

Bugattis, Rolls-Royces, and other vehicles. They were all restored and polished until they gleamed.

"I sure picked the wrong barn," Nancy said. "Well, let's—" Her words stopped cold as the hair on the back of her neck frizzed up, as if she had gotten an electric shock. Bess grabbed Nancy's arm, her nails digging in, as they heard the rear door creak open again.

Bess and Kincaid darted to the rear of a car. George was still by the blue sports car. Nancy motioned to them to get down. All four crouched between the cars. For a moment everything was still.

Then the door creaked again, and she heard it latch shut. More silence spread over the room. Who opened and closed the door? When it was closed, was the person on the inside or back outdoors? Nancy strained to hear something . . . anything.

She kept her nerves steady as she hid behind a red sports car. She leaned into the car, and her face peered back at her from the mirror of shiny paint. As she looked at her reflection, she saw a shadow form behind her.

6

The Puzzle Deepens

Nancy's breath caught in her throat as she stared into the shiny finish of the red antique sports car. She saw her own face up close. And she saw the shadow looming behind her, moving closer.

Still crouched, Nancy wheeled around to find Antoinette Francoeur standing over her. Her long face was twisted into an angry frown. Her hands were clenched into tight fists. "Who are you . . . and what are you doing in here?" she demanded.

Nancy stood slowly, her breath coming in gulps. "I'm Nancy Drew. I'm a reporter, here for your press conference."

"And what are you doing sneaking around my automobiles?" Ms. Francoeur asked. Her voice was loud as it boomed through the huge car barn.

51

"I wasn't sneaking around," Nancy said. She spoke slowly and deliberately, determined to convince the woman that she was not a threat. "My friends and I—" She stopped, saying, "Stand up, everyone." One by one, George, Bess, and Kincaid popped up from between the rows of cars.

Nancy turned back to Ms. Francoeur. "My friends and I decided not to stay for the video and buffet," she said, thinking fast. She knew she had to give the woman a reasonable excuse for being in here. But she could not let her know that she might be under investigation for rustling.

"We headed back to the parking lot, but we got turned around and ended up in the garden. As we came by the rose trellis, we noticed the back door of this building was ajar."

Antoinette Francoeur folded her long arms across her chest. She was still frowning.

"We couldn't imagine you wanted that door open. We peeked in to see if there was anything wrong—to see if there might be an intruder. When we heard the door open again, we ducked down, because we didn't know who it might be. We're so happy it was you and not an intruder."

Nancy gave her hostess a big smile, but it didn't work.

"I do not believe you," Ms. Francoeur said. "I believe *you* are the intruders. Where do you work? What is this RHI?" she demanded, reading Nancy's badge. "Is it a newspaper? A magazine?"

"We are reporters and photographers for the

River Heights Independent," Kincaid said, stepping forward boldly.

"I'm sure your organization will go far in helping animals," Nancy continued, changing the subject. "We love the logo and cover painting on your brochure. Was this painted from live models? Local bison, perhaps? They're so beautiful."

Nancy held up the brochure as she spoke.

"They really are beautiful," Bess murmured, as she and George joined Nancy and Kincaid.

"Painted from real life, yes," Ms. Francoeur said, "by a dear friend. He donated his talent for the cause. We are so grateful."

"Is he a local artist?" Nancy asked. She was trying to divert the woman by talking fast and bombarding her with questions. Maybe if she could distract Ms. Francoeur enough, the woman would overlook that she had found them trespassing. Nancy also hoped she would find out something about Lulu and Justice.

"Where did your artist find these wonderful models?" Nancy asked quickly. "Are they yours? Or animals you saved and are keeping close by until they can be released?"

Antoinette Francoeur's eyes narrowed. "Who are you really?" she asked in a low voice.

"We're members of the press who are very interested in your cause," Nancy said. "That's why we were eager to attend your press conference."

"And yet you failed to stay for the video," Ms. Francoeur said. "I think you are not telling me the truth. I want you off my property now. Go! Out of this building!"

She made a sweeping gesture with her arms, ushering Nancy and the others toward the back of the building. When they were out the door, she continued to herd them around to the parking lot. She stood watching while Kincaid unlocked her vehicle and the four climbed in.

"Let's get out of here," George said.

"I agree," Bess said, "before she changes her mind. Nancy, don't you think it's weird that she didn't call any of her guards or the police or anything when she found us snooping around?"

"Very weird," Nancy agreed. She turned and looked at Antoinette Francoeur as Kincaid pulled out onto the drive. "I was sure we were in big trouble when I saw her standing there in the car barn. I wonder why she just let us go."

"Maybe she has something to hide," George said, raising an eyebrow.

"It's possible," Nancy said. "Maybe she doesn't want the sheriff snooping around up there."

"Yeah," Kincaid said. "Maybe she *does* have something to hide—like Lulu and Justice. So, what do we do next, Nancy? I just have to do something. I can't stand the idea that my bison are trapped up there by that crazy woman."

"First of all, we don't know that she has them," Nancy said gently. "Our next step is to get more information."

"How about lunch for our next step," Bess said. "After all, we missed the buffet at Beauforêt. Remember, Kincaid, an army needs food."

"Good idea," George said. "I second it."

"We'll go to Gina's," Kincaid said as she expertly guided her vehicle down the mountain road. "Best pizza in town."

By the time they reached Gina's, it was after noon. The small restaurant was filled. "No problem," Kincaid said. "There's Clayton. Let's sit with him."

She waved to the young man they had met the night before at the Stomp. "Kincaid," he said. "I'm so glad you're here. I had a date and she stood me up. Now you can keep me company."

Clayton smiled and motioned the waitress over as Nancy and her friends sat down. "So, what's happening?" Clayton asked after they had ordered.

Kincaid briefed Clayton on Lulu and Justice's disappearance.

"Wow, that's rough," Clayton said, concern shining in his dark eyes. "I know how much they mean to you, Kinc. How come you didn't mention it at the Stomp last night?"

"Because I went there to try to escape from what's been happening," Kincaid said. "I just didn't want to talk about it last night."

"Wait till you hear about this morning," Bess said. She and Nancy told him about their experience at Beauforêt.

"Amazing," Clayton said, leaning back in his chair. "Hey, Kinc, where did you get the idea to be a detective? That's pretty awesome."

"Actually, Nancy *is* a detective," Kincaid said. "She has many cases under her belt and is in charge of our investigation. And stop calling me Kinc," she added with a mock frown. Nancy could see there was real affection between the two.

"Count me in on the case," Clayton said. "I've always thought Francoeur is half nuts. I mean, it's great to care for animals and all that, but her remedies are pretty extreme."

"Remember, we don't know that Antoinette Francoeur has any connection to the rustling," Nancy warned. "We have to have more evidence."

"But the name of her group and the picture in her logo—" Kincaid said.

"And her track record of taking animals and setting them free, no matter whom they belong to," added Clayton earnestly.

"And the fact that she didn't call the authorities when she found us hiding in her car barn," concluded Bess.

"These could all be clues pointing to her guilt . . . but they also could be coincidences," Nancy said. "We need proof, not guesses."

The pizza arrived and everyone dug in.

"So, you guys have known each other a long time," George said to Kincaid and Clayton.

"Forever, it seems," Kincaid said, her eyes twinkling. "But we got to be really good friends the summer we were interns at the geology museum."

"Yeah, that's when we started working together on archaeology digs," Clayton said. "Kinc's a real 'South Dakota Jones.'" He grinned at Kincaid. His teasing seemed to cheer her up.

"We almost caught a poacher that summer we were interns, remember?" Kincaid said.

"And he was practically one of us," Clayton pointed out.

"Sounds like a story," Bess said. She put down her pizza and leaned forward.

"Well, remember that half a mammoth jawbone I used for my national science project?" Kincaid asked. "That was the summer we worked as interns at the museum. We had an instructor."

"Jasper Stone," Clayton said, reaching for another piece of pizza.

"Right," Kincaid said. "He was a professor's assistant at the university. Well, he bragged about finding half a jawbone from a mammoth—the half—but he wouldn't show it to us."

"We thought that was pretty weird," Clayton said, "so we stayed late one night, sneaked into his desk, and looked at his find."

"It was an upper jaw," Kincaid said, "and a perfect match for my lower. You can really tell a lot about a jaw fossil by the way the teeth are worn. Jasper Stone's half was definitely the upper half of mine. And I had dug mine up on our ranch, remember? That meant he was poaching stuff from my dig and from our property."

"We confronted him about it the next day," Clayton said. "But he said he didn't know what we were talking about. He opened his desk and the jawbone was gone. We never saw it again."

"Whatever happened to him?" Nancy asked.

"I don't know," Kincaid said. "I never saw him after that summer. Did you, Clayton?"

"No," Clayton answered. "I heard a rumor that he had been caught poaching from a university dig in Wyoming, but I don't know if it's true."

"We had another interesting experience that first summer when we were interning," Clayton said, his eyes widening. "Remember?"

"I'll never forget it," Kincaid said with a shudder. "We were on a dig, and a coyote kept circling us."

"A coyote!" George said. "You're kidding."

"Nope," Clayton said. "They're all around. They usually just run away if they see people. They're not a problem unless they feel threatened," he added, taking a bite of pizza.

"But it was night and this guy just kept circling," Kincaid continued. "I got pretty nervous, so we finally left the dig. Hey, Clayton," Kincaid said, a smile lighting her face. "Why don't you come back to the ranch with us. Stay for dinner. My folks would love to see you."

"Sure," Clayton said. "I'd like that."

They all left Gina's and headed for the ranch.

Bess and George rode with Clayton. In Kincaid's vehicle, she and Nancy talked over the day's adventures as Kincaid drove.

"I want to track down the artist who did the brochure cover," Nancy said. "His name isn't on it, but we can check printers and galleries in town. Maybe someone will recognize his work."

"My mom's a sculptor in her free time and is real involved with artists around here," Kincaid said. "She volunteers at the Art Guild a few days a month and is also a docent at the art museum."

"Great!" Nancy said. "She may know who did the picture on the cover just by looking at it."

"Nancy, I really want to go back up to Beauforêt," Kincaid said. "Maybe I'm way off base, but I just have to make sure that Lulu and Justice aren't up there—that they're not going to be used as some sort of mascots for her cause."

She picked up the brochure with the painting of the bison cow and calf. Nancy could see tears in her eyes. "I'm going back up there," Kincaid said. "I think I can get into the back of the estate without being seen. You can come with me if you want, but I'll go alone if I have to."

"We'll go," Nancy assured her. "I was going to suggest it myself. I don't really think we'll find Lulu and Justice there, but something didn't feel right, and I'd like another look around."

They drove under the high wooden gate of the Turner ranch, up the drive, and into the large parking circle. Clayton's car followed closely.

As they all walked toward the ranch house, the squeal of tires filled the air behind them. Nancy wheeled around and saw a dark truck barreling up the drive.

"Somebody's sure in a hurry!" George said.

"Uh-oh," Kincaid said, running toward the house. "I think I know who it is. Dad! We've got company," she yelled through the open door. "It looks like Badger Brady."

Nancy watched warily as the truck screeched to a halt, flinging pebbles and dust in all directions. The driver's door shot open, and a man jumped out, his face red and sweaty. In his right hand he carried an ax.

"Brady!" Bill Turner called from behind Nancy. "Get off my property. Now!"

"Not until you pay for what you've done," the intruder said. "You told everybody I'm a rustler. It's a lie and you're not getting away with it."

Nancy and the others watched in horror as Brady lunged toward Mr. Turner, swinging the ax.

7

A Mountain Menace

Nancy gasped as Badger Brady swung the ax at Bill
Turner. Mr. Turner ducked, yelling, "Brady! Get
hold of yourself, man. You're going to kill somebody
with that thing."

From the corner of her eye, Nancy could see the
kitchen window. Framed in the window was Mrs.
Turner, speaking frantically into the phone. Nancy
hoped she was calling the sheriff for help.

"You have to pay, Turner," Brady yelled. "You
have to pay for spreading those lies. I didn't rustle
your stock. You've got no proof I did." He swung the
ax in a broad sweep at Mr. Turner's head.

"Dad!" Kincaid yelled. "Watch out!"

Turner ducked again, barely escaping the

61

weapon's rusty blade. "Get back, Kincaid," Mr. Turner said. "All of you—get out of the way."

Nancy, Bess, George, and Kincaid moved back toward the house. Clayton stayed near Mr. Turner, his arms up in a defensive position.

Nancy looked around for something that could help. Behind her she saw a thick rope, coiled and lying against the house. Slowly she backed up until she felt the coil against her boot heel. Holding her breath, she reached down and grasped it.

Gripping the rope behind her, she slowly walked around until she was out of Badger Brady's direct sightline. She caught Clayton's eye and nodded. Then, in one swift motion, she threw the coiled rope. Her aim was perfect, and she hit the ax squarely, knocking it out of Brady's hand.

At the same moment Clayton rushed for the ax and grabbed it up from the dusty drive. Mr. Turner lowered his head and butted Badger Brady in the midriff. With a "whoooff," Badger sailed backward and landed hard on the ground. Groaning, he tried to scramble back up, but he was too slow.

Mr. Turner grabbed Badger and stood him up against a tree. Working together, Mr. Turner and Clayton tied Badger Brady to the tree with the rope Nancy had hurled. Kincaid took the ax and leaned it against the step leading up to the porch.

"Matt will be right here," Melissa Turner said, joining the rest. "He's just a few miles down the road on another call." She looked around, asking, "Is everyone okay?"

62

"Yeah, thanks to Nancy," Clayton said, putting an arm around Nancy's shoulder. "Pretty gutsy move, throwing that rope. You're not a softball pitcher by any chance, are you? You put that one right over the plate."

"I've pitched in a few games," Nancy said, smiling. "I'm just glad no one was hurt."

"Speak for yourself," Badger Brady grumbled. He moaned again as he pulled against his restraints.

"Shut up, Brady," Mr. Turner said. "You're not going to get any sympathy here."

Nancy sat on the porch swing and took a deep breath. Clayton, Kincaid, and Mr. Turner were arguing with Badger Brady. George and Bess stood by, listening.

"Thank goodness you knocked the ax away, Nancy," Mrs. Turner said as she stepped up onto the porch.

"Kincaid was right," Nancy said. "Badger Brady's pretty nasty."

"Do you think he was the one who made the threatening phone call?" Mrs. Turner asked.

"I was just thinking about that," Nancy answered. "I really couldn't tell. The person on the phone whispered. Badger Brady has been yelling since he got here. I thought the caller had some sort of accent or unusual speech pattern, but it might have been faked. It's kind of hard to compare a whisper to Brady's angry hollering."

"I'll remind Matt about the phone call," Mrs.

Turner said. "If Badger did make it, I doubt that he'd admit it."

"I agree," Nancy said. "It sure would help if I could hear him over the phone."

"I'll talk to Matt," Mrs. Turner said. "He can set up a phone call between you two. Here he comes now," she added, stepping off the porch.

Sheriff Matt Switzer and his deputy drove up and stopped near the tree where Badger Brady was tied.

"Hey, folks," the sheriff said. "Looks like you didn't need my help after all."

Mr. and Mrs. Turner told the sheriff what had happened, with Kincaid and Clayton adding details. When they finished, the sheriff smiled at Nancy, Bess, and George, who were sitting on the porch.

"I see you're still helping us out," he said.

"That reminds me, Sheriff," Nancy said, stepping off the porch. "Have you made any connection with that hubcap we found yet? Or the tire tracks?"

"No, we haven't," the sheriff said with a narrow smile. "But we're working on it."

The sheriff untied Badger Brady. Then he put handcuffs on his wrists, arresting him for trespass and assault with a deadly weapon. "We are going to get to the bottom of this rustling, Bill," Sheriff Switzer said as he loaded Badger into the backseat of his cruiser. Then he drove off, followed by the deputy driving Badger's truck.

"Well, Clayton, I hope you're staying for supper," Mrs. Turner said with a sigh.

"You bet, Mrs. Turner," Clayton said, brushing off his jeans. "It's been a while since I've had some of your good cooking."

At an early supper the Turners, Nancy, Bess, George, and Clayton talked over the confrontation with Badger Brady. The girls also told Kincaid's parents about their experience at Antoinette Francoeur's press conference.

"So, what are all you detectives doing tomorrow?" Clayton asked as the girls walked him to his car. "Off on another search for clues?"

"I want to go out to Badger Brady's ranch and check it out," Nancy said.

"Whew," Clayton said, shaking his head. "You don't mess around, do you. You're going straight into the badger's den, right?"

"Actually, it should be pretty safe," Nancy said with a smile. "Brady will probably still be in jail."

"Did you say his place was located next to the Badlands?" Bess asked Kincaid.

"It is," Clayton said, jumping in. "And I'll be glad to drive you out there. I know just where Badger's place is. I've been on digs in that area."

"There's been incredible prehistoric stuff found around there," Kincaid said.

"I love that name—Badlands," George said. "Where is it exactly? And who named it?"

"It's an area about sixty miles east of here," Kincaid answered. "The Native Americans named it *Mako Sica,* which means 'Badlands.' The area is

65

famous all over the world among archaeologists, paleontologists, and geologists—" Kincaid said.

"It's the best fossil bed for the Oligocene period," Clayton interrupted. His enthusiasm was contagious. "That's about thirty million years ago. They've found all kinds of stuff out there—saber-toothed cats, miniature camels, and horses—"

"And the best of all," Kincaid said, her eyes wide, smiling at Clayton.

"The *titanotheres*," Clayton said, grinning. "He was awesome."

"I've never heard of the titan-o-whatever you said," Bess said. "Are you serious?"

"Absolutely," Kincaid said. "It was gigantic, a real monster. It kind of resembled a rhinoceros."

"Not something you want to run into on a dark night," Bess said with a shudder. "Or even in the daytime, for that matter."

"I'll definitely drive you there," Clayton said. "It'll be fun to snoop around for clues."

"Great," Nancy said. "Come by about noon. I've got some things to do in the morning." She was sure Clayton would be a great guide.

"See you then," Clayton said. With a big wave, he drove off.

Kincaid walked the others back to the guest cabin. "Nancy, let's go back out to Beauforêt tonight," she said. "I was thinking about it all through supper. It'll be light until eight-thirty, and I figured out a way to sneak in."

Kincaid walked to the small desk and spread out a map of the Black Hills. "Here's the Mount Rushmore Memorial," she said, pointing to a spot on the map. It was highlighted by a small picture of the carved heads of Presidents Washington, Jefferson, Theodore Roosevelt, and Lincoln.

"Beauforêt is over here," she continued, sweeping her hand over the map. "We can go to the Mount Rushmore Visitor Center, then hike through the forest a couple of miles to the back of the estate."

"We can't park at Mount Rushmore," Nancy pointed out. "If we don't get back before closing time, they'll notice the car. Is there somewhere else we can park?"

Kincaid studied the map. "Clayton's dad is a ranger, so Clayton's taken me all over this area," Kincaid said, "to places that the tourists can't get to. I'm sure that if we go up this way, we can pick up a ranger maintenance road. Then we can go up over the mountain—"

"You mean actually drive up over the presidents' heads?" Bess asked, her eyes wide.

"Well, sort of . . . behind them, actually . . . in the back," Kincaid answered with a nod. "Then we can stash the car behind a ranger maintenance shed, hike down to the visitor facilities, and then over to Beauforêt."

"Sounds good," Nancy said. "Let's do it."

Kincaid told her parents that she was taking the girls for a ride. Then she drove Nancy, Bess, and

George through Rapid City and out to the Mount Rushmore National Memorial. They drove up a two-lane winding mountain road through the dense forest and through tunnels cut in the mountains. Then they traveled under a bridge, climbed up a hairpin curve, and crossed over the same bridge.

"Look, there it is," Bess said. Through a small clearing, the four majestic presidents' heads appeared across a canyon. They were white granite and seemed to float in the air above the dark pine trees.

"Here's where the fun part starts," Kincaid said as she turned suddenly. She drove onto a winding trail up into the forest. This time it wasn't a real road. They were on a miners' road—an unmarked dirt track that the original gold miners had used.

"Have you ever driven this before?" George asked as they bounced along.

"Yes," Kincaid said. "Sort of . . . Well, not exactly," Kincaid added with a small smile. "But I've *ridden* over it. Clayton was driving. There used to be a lot of gold mines here. Most of them are abandoned and have been bulldozed over. Some are so well hidden, they'll probably never be found."

Kincaid's expert maneuvering took them at last to the ranger maintenance road. They checked in both directions, but could see no one.

"Let's hope we don't run into anyone," Nancy said. "Keep an eye out, everybody."

Although it was still light out, Kincaid had to use her headlights because the forest was so thick.

Suddenly they drove into an area in the middle of the trees that had been cleared slightly. They saw a large maintenance shed and several all-terrain vehicles.

Kincaid drove past the maintenance shed. Although the trail was shielded by trees, the girls felt as though they were riding on top of the world. Through the branches, they saw nothing but sky and the other mountains in the distance.

"Where are we?" George asked.

"We're behind the memorial," Kincaid said. "Back behind the presidents' heads."

Nancy felt an unexpected thrill. She knew they were taking a big chance sneaking up there, but she had confidence in Kincaid's experience on the mountain.

Kincaid pulled her vehicle off the trail and into the woods, stopping it behind a thick curtain of trees. The four pulled on their backpacks. Then Kincaid led them to a walking trail. A sign with an arrow pointed to the Mount Rushmore Visitor Center.

"You mean we're actually going back to civilization again?" George said.

Nancy looked at the map Kincaid had drawn of their planned hike. "Yes, but only for a minute or two. Right, Kincaid?"

"Right," Kincaid agreed, "and let's get going. I want to get to the visitor center before the show begins." Nancy and Kincaid started down the trail, followed by Bess and George.

They arrived at the visitor center in twenty minutes. Tourists were everywhere—picking up maps at the information center, buying souvenirs at the gift shops, looking at the sculptures from viewing terraces, and touring the sculptor's preserved studio. Across a canyon, the seventy-foot-high sculptures looked back at them.

"Come on," Kincaid said, starting toward a viewing trail off the main viewing terrace. "We can get to Beauforêt this way."

"Oh, let's stay a minute," George said. She stood staring across the canyon at the sculpted faces.

"They seem to be gazing back at us, don't they?" Bess said.

"Really," George agreed. "I had no idea they were so big."

"Okay, everyone," Nancy said. "Let's get going. We can come back another day and be tourists. Tonight we're going to check out Beauforêt."

Kincaid looked at Nancy with gratitude. "I just can't think of anything else but Justice and Lulu now," she said.

"I understand," Nancy said, "and I'd like to get going before it gets too dark." As she spoke, the crowd began moving away from the terrace and gathering at the elevators and stairs that led down to the amphitheater.

"They're getting ready for the show," Kincaid said. "It's a perfect time for us to disappear."

Single file, they headed up the trail that led to

70

the rear of Antoinette Francoeur's estate. Kincaid led the way, with Nancy close behind. George offered to be last, to make sure they weren't being followed.

Nancy tried to sidestep twigs so there would be no unexpected crackle in the hushed forest. She felt a sense of excitement and anticipation as they followed the trail through the thick trees.

It got darker and darker as they moved away from the visitor center. Nancy and Kincaid retrieved their flashlights from their backpacks.

Behind them, Nancy could hear faint words and music over a sound system. Ahead, there was nothing but an occasional rustle as a bird flew through the dense branches above them or a small animal scampered below.

Nancy's mind was racing with plans. We should head straight for the second barn in case the missing buffalo are there, she thought. We also need to check the auto barn again. There were cars and trucks that hadn't been restored yet. It wouldn't hurt to check their hubcaps. Then we could—

Nancy's thoughts halted instantly when she heard the sound and Kincaid stopped abruptly. Nancy threw an arm out behind her to motion the others to stop. Then she heard the sound again. A few yards ahead of them on the trail, someone moved quickly, then slowed. Then there was just one step. Then silence.

For a moment Nancy heard only her own pulse, throbbing in her ears. Then she heard another footstep. She darted off the path, motioning the others to follow her lead. Naturally hidden by the forest, they crouched and waited.

Watching and listening for several minutes, they heard nothing. Her skin tingling from her head to her feet, Nancy finally stepped out onto the path. It curved to the right, so she could see only about three yards ahead.

She made her way to the bend in the path, then held her breath. Against the dark of the dense trees, she could just make out an even darker silhouette. Someone was waiting for them around the curve.

8

Bess Tumbles for Lincoln

Nancy's thoughts raced. If I heard him coming, he—or she—probably heard us too, Nancy thought. So it's too late to duck back into the forest. She motioned for Bess, George, and Kincaid to stay back. Whoever it is probably doesn't know how many of us there are, Nancy reasoned. She knew if she needed help, surprise would be a big advantage for her.

Nancy took a deep breath, then asked firmly, "Who's there?"

There was no answer, but the person took a step closer. Nancy was pretty sure it was a man. He was very tall and slim and dressed in a Mount Rushmore uniform. His face was almost completely concealed by the wide bill of a baseball cap. It looked as if tufts of light hair bristled around the ears.

"Who is it?" Nancy asked, firmly holding her ground. "Who's there?"

The person took another couple of steps closer. He—or she—seemed to favor the right leg and limped slightly.

"Nancy, be careful," Kincaid said, popping out from behind a tree.

The stranger jumped with surprise, then stepped back when he saw Kincaid.

"Outta my way," he grumbled through clenched teeth, glaring at Nancy and the others. Then he shoved roughly past them, knocking Kincaid to the ground.

George and Bess rushed out to help Nancy pull Kincaid to her feet. They looked down the path back toward the visitor center, but the stranger was out of sight.

"Are you all right?" Bess asked Kincaid.

"Yeah, I guess so," she answered, and stood, brushing pine needles from her jeans.

"I wonder who that was," George said, looking down the path.

"Kincaid, did you get a look at him?" Nancy asked.

"No," Kincaid answered. "It all happened so fast, I didn't get a good look. I think it was a man, though."

"But you didn't recognize him?" Nancy asked.

"Not really," Kincaid said, adjusting her backpack.

"What is it, Nancy?" Bess asked. "There's something you're after, isn't there?"

"I don't know," Nancy said, her eyes narrowing as she remembered the encounter. "It almost looked as if he recognized Kincaid when she jumped out. When you popped up, he looked right at you, then rushed away. I know you startled him, but there was something more in his expression."

"I wish I'd gotten a better look at him," Kincaid said. "I wonder if it *was* someone I know—that's really scary."

"Well, he seems to be gone now, so let's get back on the trail to Beauforêt," Nancy said, heading out. Soon they reached the back of Antoinette Francoeur's property.

"There," Kincaid said triumphantly. "I knew it. Look. There's the car barn, the parking lot. The house is up ahead."

Even though the estate was more open than the forest, there was little moonlight. So it was dark. It was also very quiet. There was no sign of anyone around the grounds.

"I want to check something in the antique car barn first," Nancy whispered.

"We've already been there," Kincaid said, obviously disappointed. "I want to look in the other barns and outbuildings. If Lulu and Justice are up here, I want to find them."

75

Nancy could see that Kincaid was determined and she wasn't going to change her mind. "Okay," Nancy said. "Bess, you and Kincaid go to the other barn. Wait there for George and me. Now listen, everybody. We may not see anyone right now, but we know she has guards. Keep out of sight and be quiet."

Nancy watched as Bess and Kincaid darted toward the other large building. Then she and George moved quickly to the rear door of the car barn. Nancy used her lock pick to open it.

She waited for a minute to see if she had roused the attention of any guard, but all remained quiet. Cautiously, she and George stepped inside. One faint ray of moonlight shone through a window at the front of the building. They followed it to the unrestored automobiles in the corner.

These cars were in various stages of restoration. Some needed just a paint job, some needed tires or windows. Nancy pulled out her flashlight.

"What are we looking for?" George asked.

"Hubcaps," Nancy said. "The one we found at Lulu and Justice's shelter was unusual, remember?"

"Mm-hmm," George said with a nod. "It looked as if it had a design in the center, but I couldn't tell what it was."

Nancy laid her flashlight on the hood of a car. Then she reached in her backpack and took out a piece of paper. It was the pencil rubbing she had made of the hubcab.

"It was an unusual hubcap," Nancy said. "And Antoinette Francoeur collects unusual cars. That hubcap was rusty and dented, and some of these cars are in similar shape."

The two checked all the wheels of the cars waiting to be restored.

"Nothing," George said flatly. "Well, I guess we'd better go. Bess and Kincaid will think we've been caught—or something worse."

Disappointed, Nancy flashed the light beam around the large room. "Wait a minute," she said. "What's that?"

An old truck sat in the corner by the large garage door. Nancy and George hurried across the room. The truck wasn't an antique, but it was old—and it was very well used.

Nancy stooped down to check the wheels. Three had hubcaps that were dented and rusty like the one they had found. In the center of each was an indistinguishable design. The fourth tire boasted a brand-new hubcap. Shiny and silver in the flashlight beam, the center of the hubcap was etched with a fleur-de-lis pattern.

"Of course," Nancy said. "The fleur-de-lis. It's an iris design and was used a lot on armor and in banners in France. It was a symbol of the monarchy." She felt the tire treads. "Mmm," she added. "This truck has been used recently. And look at the dirt caked in the treads. It looks like the clay soil on the Turners' ranch out by Lulu and Justice's shelter."

"Maybe Kincaid was right all along," George said. "Ms. Francoeur *did* take her bison."

"Let's get to the other barn," Nancy said. "Maybe they found something." She stuffed the flashlight and pencil rubbing into her backpack. Quickly they left the car barn and headed across the drive to the other large building.

The door was unlocked. Inside, the sweetish odor of goats and dairy cows mixed with the fresh scent of hay and alfalfa. Bess and Kincaid were just inside the door, waiting. In the faint moonlight, Nancy could see the disappointment on their faces. "Nothing," Bess said.

"We had a little more luck," George said. "Tell them, Nancy."

Nancy told them about the truck, the hubcap, and the fresh dirt. "It sure looks as though someone drove that truck out to Lulu and Justice's shelter," Nancy concluded.

"Then where are they?" Kincaid said. "There aren't any other buildings on the estate that could hold them. There's no pasture. Where could they be?" She sighed. "I say we go confront the woman. Tell her what we found and ask her where my bison are."

"Not a good idea," Nancy said. "Let's have Sheriff Switzer take care of it. We can tell him about the hubcaps on that truck. Having the sheriff ask her why she was trespassing on your ranch will get better results than we will—especially since we've been caught trespassing on *her* property."

"Good point, Nancy," Bess said. She put an arm around Kincaid's shoulders. "Come on," she said. "Nancy's right. Let's get back to the car."

They retraced their steps along the nature trail back to the Mount Rushmore Visitor Center. "Nancy, how can we tell the sheriff that we saw those hubcaps at Beauforêt without telling him we were there?" Kincaid asked.

"You call him tomorrow morning. Tell him we were there for the press conference and we saw the hubcaps," Nancy said. "He'll assume the two things happened at the same time."

"Good plan," Kincaid murmured, nodding. By the time they reached the visitor center, it was nearly midnight and everything was closed. From the shelter of the trees, they could see two rangers drinking coffee and talking on one of the viewing terraces. There was no one else visible. There were no clouds now and a half-moon shone down on the massive granite heads.

Concealed by the dense forest, they hiked back up to their all-terrain vehicle. "Well, I don't know about you guys, but I'm glad to be heading back," Bess said as Kincaid started the motor.

Kincaid had begun to maneuver the vehicle onto the ranger road when suddenly she stopped and turned to the others. "There's one more thing we have to do while we're here," she said, opening her door. "Something that will help us remember this night forever."

"What's that?" George asked with a yawn.

"Where are we going?" Bess asked warily. "I have a funny feeling about this." They stood in the clearing near the maintenance shed.

"We're going to stand on the heads," Kincaid said, her voice brimming with excitement. "Clayton and I did it once. It's such a thrill. You really feel like you're on top of the world. It's just a short walk. We won't actually go onto the heads. I'm afraid the rangers would see us, but we'll get close to it. Come on."

Without waiting for the others, she headed off into the trees. Nancy, George, and Bess followed. Abruptly they left the shelter of the trees and were in the open. Nancy's heart did a somersault as she took in the breathtaking view. Even in the dark, she could see the outlines of mountains for miles in all directions. She had a spooky feeling knowing that they were actually above the presidents' heads.

"I thought you said it was just a short walk," George grumbled as they made their way down the steep rocky path.

Nancy and Bess were walking side by side. Suddenly Bess's ankle twisted, and she fell heavily into Nancy. Nancy grabbed for her friend, but Bess slipped away.

"Oh no," Bess cried as she tumbled. "I can't . . . catch myself . . . somebody . . . grab me."

"Hang on, Bess," Nancy yelled as she and

George half ran and half slid down to their friend.

Nancy felt a cold clammy sweat spread over her as she watched in terror as her friend slid onto the cliff above Lincoln's head.

9

A Few Pieces Fit

Nancy, George, and Kincaid raced forward to see Bess tumble onto the cliff above Lincoln's head. Finally she came to a stop in a jumbled heap.

"Hold on, Bess," Nancy called in a loud whisper. Her voice seemed to disappear in the vast open air at the top of the mountain. "It's okay, we're here."

"We're here, Bess," George echoed as she and Kincaid moved up beside Nancy.

"Owwww," Bess moaned. "My shoulder. I think I hurt my shoulder when I landed."

"Don't move," Nancy said. "I'm coming to get you. Try to stay still and keep your voice down. We'll be in even more trouble if the rangers down at the visitor center hear us." Nancy sat down on the rocky ground and scooted down to where Bess lay and helped her friend to sit up.

As she looked around, Nancy felt a sudden moment of weightlessness. Sitting on top of Lincoln's head made her feel a little off balance.

"Do you want us to come down there?" George called.

"No, stay where you are," Nancy said. "We can make it." Their arms looped together, the two crawled back up the rocky incline to where George and Kincaid waited.

Bess stood up and moved her arm around several times. "Ummph," she muttered. "It hurts."

"We'd better get you to a doctor," Nancy said. "You probably should have your arm x-rayed."

"Can you move it?" George asked.

Bess gingerly shrugged her shoulder. "It's okay, I guess," she said. "It just hurts."

Gently prodding Bess's arm, Kincaid said, "I'll bet it's only bruised."

"Just get me home," Bess said. "I'll be okay. I feel better just thinking about that cabin bathtub and bed."

"Well, be sure to let us know if you think you need to see a doctor tomorrow," Kincaid said.

"I will, I will," Bess said, walking slowly to the car. "Well, you were right, Kincaid," Bess concluded, as they drove down the winding ranger road. "That *was* a thrill."

* * *

83

Wednesday morning Bess was sore and a little bruised, but she felt pretty good, considering the tumble she had taken. She insisted she didn't need to see a doctor.

"Okay, then, we're still on to go out to Badger Brady's today," Nancy said, checking her watch. "Clayton won't be here until noon. That's about an hour and a half from now. I'm going to talk to Kincaid's mom about the artist for Antoinette Francoeur's brochure." She grabbed the press kit they had gotten at Beauforêt and headed across the path toward the Turner house.

Melissa Turner was working at her desk when Nancy entered the house. Mrs. Turner was dressed in leather jeans and boots and a red shirt that set off her pale skin and dark hair.

"Nancy," Mrs. Turner said. "I was just thinking about the case. Matt says Badger is still insisting he's not the rustler." Mrs. Turner leaned forward, worry creasing her forehead. "We've got to figure out who the rustler is—and soon, or we may lose our ranch. Do you have any ideas?"

"Actually, I was hoping you could help me out," Nancy said.

"Sure," Mrs. Turner answered. She leaned back in her chair and urged Nancy to sit in the soft plush love seat next to her desk.

Nancy opened the press kit and took out the Justice for Animals brochure and other materials. "Take a look at this illustration," she said, offering the brochure to Mrs. Turner.

Mrs. Turner studied the picture of the two bison. "This looks like the work of one of our Art Guild members, a local artist. He's a Native American whose tribal name means All Bright Winter Moon, but he goes by Jack Allbright."

"And you think he might have done this illustration?" Nancy asked.

"I'd bet on it," Melissa Turner said. "He does watercolors and has a really distinctive brushstroke. Wow! These look like Lulu and Justice."

"Kincaid thought so, too," Nancy said. "How can I get hold of Jack Allbright?" Nancy said. "I want to ask him about this illustration."

"Well, let me see," Mrs. Turner said. "I should have his number right here. Yes, here it is. You want me to call and introduce you?"

"That would be wonderful," Nancy said.

Mrs. Turner dialed the number and waited. Then she crinkled her nose up at Nancy, saying "Answering machine." She waited a few more moments, then said, "Jack? Hi, this is Melissa Turner. I just saw the brochure for Justice for Animals. Congratulations on your cover work! We have a visitor here—a friend of Kincaid's—who'd like to talk to you about the illustration. Her name is Nancy Drew. Give us a call when you get in, please. Thanks."

She hung up and turned back to Nancy. "There you go," she said. "I'm sure he'll call as soon as he gets in. I'll let you know. By the way, I talked to Matt about setting up a call with Badger Brady so you could check out his phone voice. Matt said just call him and he'll take care of it."

"Thanks a lot," Nancy said.

"Let me know if there's anything more I can do," Mrs. Turner said. "I feel so frustrated. We've got to get to the bottom of this, Nancy."

"We will," Nancy assured her. She gathered up the press kit and headed back to the guest cabin, determined to find out who was causing so much trouble for the Turners.

Kincaid was waiting at the cabin when Nancy walked in. "I called Sheriff Matt," Kincaid said. "I told him about the hubcaps. He's going to take the one we found up to Beauforêt and question Antoinette Francoeur himself."

"Good," Nancy said. "I talked to your mom, and she thinks the brochure was illustrated by a local artist named Jack Allbright. She left a message on his answering machine to call us when he gets back. By the way, she thinks the buffalo look like Lulu and Justice, too."

"What if it is, Nancy?" Kincaid asked. "Maybe that's proof that Miss Francoeur took them."

"Let's wait till we talk to Allbright," Bess said. "Don't get your hopes up."

"Bess, we have two more calls to make," Nancy said, "and you have to make one of them. I'm afraid Antoinette Francoeur would recognize my voice from our confrontation in her auto barn."

Nancy reached for the phone. "Kincaid, what's the name of a good lunchroom or tearoom in town?" she asked. Then she coached Bess on what to say to Ms. Francoeur.

Bess dialed the number printed on the Justice for Animals brochure. "Antoinette Francoeur, please," she said into the receiver at last. She listened for a moment, then said, "This is Bess Marvin. I'm calling about starting a young adult chapter of Justice for Animals."

She waited for another minute, then smiled at the others. "Ah, Ms. Francoeur," Bess said into the phone. "I am so excited about your organization— and about the opportunity to speak to you.

"In fact, a few friends and I are organizing a young adult league for the liberation of animals. We plan to visit schools and carry our message to students. We've also been thinking of affiliating ourselves with Justice for Animals. Perhaps we could meet tomorrow at RuthAnn's Tea Room to talk."

Bess paused to listen, then spoke again. "How about lunch? One o'clock would be perfect. We'll meet you then. And thank you."

"She'll recognize us as soon as she walks in," George said. "She'll be furious."

"Maybe," Nancy said. "But I think she really believes in her cause. If we can convince her we do, too, we might win her confidence."

"And then what?" Kincaid asked.

"I'm going to question her. Find out about that hubcap. Maybe we can get some answers."

"But think about what that shelter looked like, Nancy," George said. "Do you really believe she would tear it apart like that? It was a mess. She had to have help."

"I agree," Nancy said. "All we know is that one of her vehicles may have been there. We don't know who might have been driving, why they were there, or what they did while they were there. That's what we need to find out."

"I believe that Miss Francoeur took Lulu and Justice," Kincaid said.

"As Nancy said, we don't have any real proof," Bess said.

"But don't you see," Kincaid continued. "I have to hope she took them because then at least I know they're okay. She wouldn't hurt them." Kincaid's voice dropped as she spoke her next words. "If Badger took them, I'll never see them again."

Nancy felt sorry for the young woman. She knew Kincaid was right. She also agreed with Clayton that Brady was the more likely culprit. But if Badger Brady is the rustler, she asked herself, what was Antoinette Francoeur's hubcap doing near Lulu and Justice's pen?

"You said you had two more calls, Nancy," George said. "Bess made one. How about the other?"

"I want to call the sheriff," Nancy said. "Mrs. Turner said she'd have him rig up a phone call between Badger Brady and me. I want to see if I recognize his phone voice." She checked her watch. "I think we still have time to get it done before Clayton comes to take us to Brady's ranch."

"By the way," Kincaid added, "I told my folks you're driving out to see the Badlands. I don't think they'd be too thrilled to know you were poking around Badger Brady's. They'd be worried."

"Good idea," George said.

"Also," Kincaid said in a soft voice, "I'm not going with you."

"What?" Bess said. "Why not, Kincaid?"

"Nancy, I'm sure you know what you're doing," Kincaid said. "Looking for clues is really important." She sighed. "But I want to find Lulu and Justice first," she continued. "Then I can worry about who took them. I want to ride along the perimeter of the ranch today. I know Lulu, and in my heart I know there's no chance that she just wandered off. But I have to check, just in case."

"Do you mind if I stay with Kincaid?" Bess asked. "I can keep her company and help her look."

"Not at all," Nancy said. "It's a good idea."

Nancy dialed the sheriff's number, then asked for Matt Switzer. She felt a ripple across her shoulders as the deputy spoke. Slowly she hung up the phone and turned to the others.

"Sheriff Switzer is in the hospital," she reported. "He was shot by Badger Brady when Brady escaped from jail!"

10

Bad Times at the Badlands

"Matt's been shot?" Kincaid said, her face pale. "How is he?"

"He's in surgery right now," Nancy said.

"When did it happen?" George asked. "And how?"

"About an hour ago," Nancy said. "Brady's brother helped him escape. He's the one who actually shot Sheriff Switzer."

"I told you about his family," Kincaid reminded them. "They're nothing but trouble. I have to tell my folks," she added, racing to the door.

"I'm still going to Brady's ranch today," Nancy said. She felt a flush of determination surge through her. "Actually, it should be pretty safe. It's probably the last place he'd go."

"Are you sure?" Bess asked, worried. "I don't know, Nancy. If he's escaped, he doesn't have much to lose."

"I know, but I still want to look around out there," Nancy said.

Nancy and George gathered up their backpacks and headed for the ranch house.

Clayton arrived a few minutes later. The others brought him up to date. He seemed glad that Nancy and George still wanted to go to Badger Brady's.

"Now, you be careful in the Badlands," Melissa Turner said.

"Oh, we will," George said sheepishly. Mr. and Mrs. Turner left and Kincaid and Bess helped Nancy, George, and Clayton load Clayton's car.

It took them twenty minutes to pack up all the provisions Kincaid and Clayton thought they needed. They took sandwiches, fruit, sodas, chips, gloves, boots, binoculars, flashlights, cameras, a cell phone, rope, knives, a first aid kit with snakebite medicine, extra gas, and lots of water.

"By the way," Clayton said, rearranging the boots. "My dad tells me that some young women were spotted on the mountain near Lincoln's head last night. He asked me if I knew anything about it or them. I told him I didn't—and it was the truth. But it sure sounded like someone I took up there once," he added with a grin.

"Shhh," Kincaid warned him. "It was us, okay? Nancy and George will tell you about it on the drive out to Badger's. We managed to get back in last night without my parents' finding out about it. Let's keep it that way."

Bess peeked in the window of Clayton's car. "I don't know where you expect anyone to sit," she said. "This car's a mess."

Clayton leaned into the backseat and swept papers, rocks, and books into a bag. More stuff covered the floor and the front seat.

"Clayton is even more into fossils and prehistoric digs than I am," Kincaid said, "as you can see."

"Wow," George said, picking up a small skull. "What's this?"

"That's a prehistoric miniature camel skull," Clayton answered. "I found it out near where we're going today, actually."

"In the Badlands?" George asked, turning the skull around in her hand.

"No," Clayton said. "If I had I couldn't have kept it. It's against federal law to take fossils or plants or anything out of the Badlands." He shoved more stuff into the corner of the backseat.

"Old-timers talk of seeing wagonloads of prehistoric fossils carted out of there," he continued. "But it's been illegal since it became a national park in 1939. That doesn't stop some people, of course. Poachers are always being caught in there. It's such a wild area, and it's hard to keep track of everyone."

He lifted a cooler of sodas into the car. "I dug

that skull up near the Badlands, though," he said, "on a friend's property."

"Hey, what's this? This looks like a whole *bag* of bones," George added, picking up a large lumpy plastic bag from the floor of the backseat. She and Bess looked inside the bag.

"Not camel bones, though," Bess added with a laugh.

"Nope. These are more from the prehistoric rawhide-chew-osaur," George said. She pulled a dog's chew toy from the bag. It was made of rawhide and shaped like a thick bone.

"For Brutus, right?" Kincaid said. "Clayton's got this monster Great Dane named Brutus," she added as Clayton nodded. "This huge bag will probably be gone in a week." She threw the bag of chew toys onto the floor of the backseat.

"Okay, pile in," Clayton said.

Nancy climbed into the back, and George rode next to Clayton in the front as they left for Badger Brady's.

On the drive Nancy and George caught Clayton up on what they'd seen the night before at Beauforêt. They told him about finding the truck with the matching hubcaps and that the sheriff was going to question Antoinette Francoeur.

George filled him in on the most treacherous part of the evening's activities—the ride over Mount Rushmore.

"Kincaid is fearless," Clayton said, shaking his

head. "And her mom and dad are really great. We have to help them find out who's doing this."

"With Nancy in charge, we will," George said.

"Well, I hate to say this," Clayton said, "but I just can't figure Antoinette Francoeur for a rustler. Now Badger Brady, on the other hand, fits the bill perfectly."

Nancy studied the map she had taken out of her backpack. "Kincaid marked an old road here that she thinks leads to Brady's," she said.

"This is all the Buffalo Gap National Grasslands," Clayton said, sweeping his arm around. "The Pine Ridge Reservation is over there." He pointed to a spot in the distance.

"I'm going to take the scenic route to Badger Brady's and drive through the Badlands," he said.

"Good," George said. "That way we can truthfully tell the Turners we were there."

"Okay," Nancy said. "As long as it doesn't take too much extra time. I really want to get to Brady's as soon as possible."

"Actually, it's just as quick to go through the Badlands as it is to go around," Clayton said. "The trick is not getting too sidetracked by the beauty and weirdness of the place."

When they first reached the Badlands, Nancy could hardly believe her eyes. Clayton drove onto Sage Creek Rim Road and pulled into a vast natural fantasyland—a wild, unexpected part of South Dakota.

"There's no place on earth like this," Clayton

said, gesturing with a broad sweep of his arm. Some parts looked like the Southwest, with deep, rough-cut canyons and gorges. Other areas resembled the surface of the moon, with softly rounded craters and pits. Still other areas looked like nothing Nancy or George had ever seen.

In the distance, on the upper grasslands, a herd of antelope and some prong-horned sheep grazed. Overhead, a golden eagle soared from a huge canyon up to mountainlike spires and narrow pyramids of rock that all ended in rounded-off points.

"It's almost as if we're seeing the ruins of some ancient walled city," Nancy said. "Only everything is made of rock."

"And look at the colors," George added. The rock walls were layered in hues of blue, purple, gold, and reddish orange.

As they drove, they passed a huge community of prairie dogs that had built a town of their own. Hundreds of mounds and humps rose from the ground. The little animals popped in and out of their homes in frantic bursts of activity.

The landscape was so unreal, Nancy felt as if she were in a dream. As she watched out the window, a herd of bison came into view. They were grazing in a great basin surrounded by domes and pyramids of rock.

Clayton drove around until they reached an unearthly sight—thousands of pointed spires of rock that reached sixty feet into the sky.

"This is so wild," George said. "Let's stop—just for a minute."

"This area is called the Pinnacles," Clayton said as the three stepped out of the car at a lookout spot. There was only one other vehicle parked there—a dusty black pickup truck.

"Come on," George said. "Just a short hike. I have to see what it feels like to be standing down at the bottom."

Before anyone could stop her, she had started down a rough path that led to the floor of the dense formation of huge pointed rocks. Within minutes she was out of sight, hidden among the tall spires. Skidding and sliding, Nancy and Clayton followed her trail, weaving in and out of the tall pointed columns.

The Pinnacles were so dense, Nancy caught sight of George for only a few seconds at a time. Then as soon as she appeared, she rounded another column and was hidden again. It was almost like being in a huge prehistoric maze.

Nancy felt a little disoriented as they wound around and through the Pinnacles. For a second, she wondered how they would ever find their way back to the car. She tried to find a landmark to help her pinpoint a position. But when she looked up, all she saw were hundreds of pointed rock spires and small patches of blue sky. Ahead and all around was nothing but the Pinnacles.

After twenty minutes of winding and weaving, Nancy did spot George. She was sitting on a small ledge a few yards up the side of one of the Pinnacles. A pair of binoculars hung around her neck. When George saw Nancy and Clayton, she put a finger to her lips to motion them to be quiet. Then she gestured for Nancy to climb up and join her.

The ledge was small so only Nancy joined George. George handed Nancy the binoculars and pointed through the Pinnacles.

From the ledge, Nancy had a better perspective than she had at ground level. As soon as she had adjusted the binoculars, she ignored George's pointing finger and looked back the way they had come. It helped her get her bearings, and she was able to plan a route to take back to the car.

Then Nancy swung the binoculars around to where George was pointing. Two men were at the base of the Pinnacles, about thirty yards away. She adjusted the lens so she could see more clearly. The men were working with small tools—a spade, a whiskbroom, an ax. They seemed to be digging near the base of a pinnacle. They were completely concealed by the spires of rock from almost all angles.

Nancy checked the clothes the men were wearing. "They're not wearing rangers' uniforms," she murmured to George, and reached into her backpack and pulled out a camera. She adjusted the zoom lens and snapped a couple of shots of the two men. Then she dropped her camera in her backpack and took back the binoculars for another look.

"Hey, what's going on?" Clayton called from below. "What are you looking at?"

Clayton's voice echoed through the Pinnacles. Nancy motioned for Clayton to be silent with one hand but kept the binoculars close to her eyes with the other. As she watched, the men stood and turned. They wheeled around from side to side. Then one of them turned to face the ledge where Nancy and George sat.

Nancy held her breath as she watched the man raise an arm and point a finger right at her. His eyes stared at her through the lenses of her binoculars.

11

Braving the Badger's Lair

Nancy gasped because the man's expression was angry and determined. Nancy leaped into action. "We've been spotted," she said to George. "We've got to get out of here."

As they scrambled down from the ledge, Nancy explained what they'd seen to Clayton.

"Sounds like poachers," Clayton said.

"Follow me," Nancy said. "I'm pretty sure I can get us out of here."

She wound back through the Pinnacles along the route she planned when she first looked through the binoculars. She could hear George and Clayton following close behind. She could also hear pounding feet farther back. She knew it was the men she had seen, and felt that she and her friends were in danger. They had to get to the car as soon as possible.

She couldn't get the picture of the one man's expression out of her mind. It spurred her on. "Faster," she called back to Clayton and George. "They're right behind us."

They finally reached the path to the car, and hopped, jumped, and clawed their way back up to the lookout point. Within minutes, they were in the car with the motor started. As they pulled away, Nancy could see the two men halfway up the path.

"Drive," she ordered Clayton, getting out the cell phone. "Get us to a ranger station—quick!" They had gotten a brochure when they entered the Badlands. Nancy called the number listed on the brochure.

At the ranger station, Clayton and a ranger studied a large map of the Badlands that was hanging on the wall.

"Here's the ledge where Nancy and George sat," Clayton said, indicating a spot on the map. "So the poachers must have been here," he added, pointing to a spot on the valley floor that would be about thirty yards away.

"I took some photographs while we were up on the ledge," Nancy said. "I'll send you copies when I get them developed if you'll give me your exact address."

She pictured the men in her mind's eye. "One of them was tall and thin, wore jeans and a jeans jacket, and had grayish hair. I had a better look at the other one," she continued, remembering the menacing face she spotted through the binoculars. "He was shorter and stocky with long bushy dark hair and thick eyebrows. He wore a brown windbreaker and jeans and had a canvas hat on, with the brim turned down all the way around."

Clayton told them about the truck that had been parked at the lookout spot, and George gave them the license number.

"They're probably still around," Nancy pointed out. "They had to go back to get their tools and anything they might have dug up."

One of the rangers nodded, saying, "You know, I thought we'd had enough excitement around here for one day with that crazy Frenchwoman and her group marching around."

"Are you talking about Antoinette Francoeur?" Nancy said. "Is she here today?"

"Yep," the ranger said. "She and her organization are picketing outside our museum. They want to close the Badlands down to tourists and leave it for the animals. She got a permit, so we have to let her do her thing."

The rangers thanked them, and one left to try to find the men Nancy and George had seen. After leaving numbers where they could be contacted, Nancy, George, and Clayton returned to their car.

"Mmmm," George said, opening the cooler. "A soda would be great right now." She passed one back to Nancy and opened one for Clayton. Then she passed sandwiches around.

"Our real work today hasn't even started," Nancy said. She took a bite of sandwich and washed it down with a cold swallow of soda. She hadn't realized how hungry and thirsty she was. "How far to Badger Brady's, Clayton?"

"I'll get my bearings as soon as we get through this stretch," Clayton answered as he pulled out of the Badlands and back into farm and ranch land.

He drove awhile longer and finally pulled onto a narrow unmarked dirt road. "Badger's place is in this direction. I've used this road when I went on digs around this area. We should be circling around his ranch in a few miles."

The road finally stopped at an eight-foot-high barbed wire fence that was peppered with hand-printed signs. "This must be the place," George said in a low voice.

Stop! announced one of the signs. Trespassers Will Be Shot! warned another. Stay Out! demanded the third.

They sat for a minute, just watching. There was no sign of anyone—the ranch appeared to be abandoned.

"I don't see any buffalo," George said, her voice in a whisper.

"He's probably got several hundred acres," Clayton said. "They could just be out of sight."

"Well, there's where I want to go," Nancy said, pointing to a cluster of old wood buildings in the distance. She opened her car door. "Let's walk around the fence for a while—see if we can find an opening." She reached for her backpack and started walking.

Nancy, George, and Clayton followed the barbed wire fence. "Here," Nancy said, running ahead. "How about here?"

"It seems Badger Brady's been too busy to maintain his fence," Clayton said. Two of the three lines of barbed wire were twisted and tangled together. The third lay on the ground.

Clayton took a pair of battered leather gloves from his vest pocket and pulled them on. He held the tangled mass of wire up as Nancy and George slid under and into Badger Brady's pasture.

Clayton passed Nancy the gloves, and she held the wire while he ducked under. Then the three darted to a large bushy shrub. They were hidden and protected there while they planned their next move.

"That's probably the house," Nancy said, nodding toward a wooden farmhouse near a grove of trees. The house was gray, and even from a distance, she could tell it needed repairs and paint.

"Yeah," Clayton agreed, "and there's the barn and the outbuildings."

"Let's go," Nancy whispered. Using shrubs for cover, she led the others up to the grove of trees near the house.

"I don't see anyone, Nancy," George said in a low voice.

Nancy nodded as she gestured to the others to stay put while she crept along the house. Reaching a large window next to the front door, Nancy crouched low beneath the glass. Cautiously, she raised her head until she was barely able to peek inside.

She was looking through a sheer, dirty curtain into the living room. It was sparsely furnished with old, raggedy-looking furniture and a small desk in the corner. A single rug lay on the wooden floor. She could see through a large archway into the dining room, which had a table, three chairs, and a cabinet. There was no one in sight.

She crouched back down and crept back to George and Clayton. "I don't see anyone," she said.

"I haven't heard any barking," Clayton pointed out. "He must not have any guard dogs."

"Let's try the door," George urged.

The three crept up to the front door. Nancy tried the knob. It was unlocked. As she pushed, a low whine creaked from the rusty hinges. Nancy held her breath, but no one responded to the opening door.

Nancy led the others inside. The stony quiet was almost unreal. There was no sound at all—not a bird singing, not even any leaves rustling.

Nancy moved quickly through the living room to the old desk in the corner. There were a few papers on the desktop, but nothing significant. She dropped her backpack on the floor and looked through the desk drawers. Again, there was nothing that seemed important to the rustling case.

Behind her, George and Clayton checked the floor and under the sofa and chair cushions. They, too, came up empty-handed.

A quick search of the rest of the downstairs was just as disappointing. The kitchen pantry had a few canned soups. A jar of pickles and a plastic squirt bottle of mustard were the only residents of the humming refrigerator. In the sink were a few dishes encrusted with dried bits of food.

By now, they were sure they were alone in the house. They had been there nearly a half hour and no one had appeared.

Nancy grabbed her backpack and led George and Clayton upstairs. There were three bedrooms and a bathroom. One bedroom was completely bare, and one had only a bed and a chest. The blankets on the bed were rumpled. The third bedroom had a chair and a sofa that sloped to the right on two broken legs.

"Hey, look at this," Clayton said. He reached under the bed and pulled out a large, oval dome-shaped piece of rock.

"It's a rock, right?" George said, walking over to him.

"Look closer," Clayton said, taking her hand and passing it lightly over the surface.

"It looks almost like a shell or a—" She took it over to the window to get a better view. "It's a fossil, isn't it? Is it a turtle shell? A really old one?"

"That's right," Clayton said. "And it's old, all right—about thirty million years old. Must have been found right around here."

Nancy walked out of the bedroom. "I saw a door under the staircase," she said. "Let's check it out. It might be a closet or a door to a basement."

They stepped into the upstairs hall. Nancy led, her ears straining for any sound that might indicate they weren't alone. "Remember, Badger Brady is running around loose," she said, her voice hushed. "I don't think he'll come back here, but you never know."

"It looks to me as if Badger's already been here," Clayton said with a shrug. "And cleared out anything important. What are we looking for exactly?"

"Anything that might help prove Badger Brady has been rustling the Turners' bison," George answered, as they walked down the staircase. "Right, Nancy?"

"Yes," Nancy said. "Or that might prove he *hasn't* been rustling," Nancy added.

The three stepped onto the main floor and walked around to the door beneath the staircase. Slowly Nancy turned the knob. The door opened to reveal a staircase leading to the basement. It was dimly lit, so Nancy reached around the wall until she found a light switch. She flicked it, but nothing happened.

106

"Must be a bad bulb," George mumbled.

Nancy took a flashlight from her backpack. Clayton followed her lead and turned on his flashlight, too. Nancy slung her backpack over one shoulder and started down the stairs. The two flashlight beams showed rickety, splintered steps leading to a basement draped in cobwebs.

Nancy felt a tingle as she made her way down. "Be careful," George whispered from behind.

When they reached the dirt floor, Nancy and Clayton swung their light beams around. Just then Nancy heard a board creak above them, and suddenly the basement door was slammed shut. They heard loud scraping and shuffling noises, and then it was still again.

Clayton ran up the stairs and pushed the door. "It's locked or something," he said. "It gives a little when I push, but it seems to be jammed. I can't get it to open."

An odd sound caught Nancy's attention from a corner of the basement. Every nerve jumped to attention as she listened. It was a soft, low, throaty rumble. Nancy felt a prickle at the back of her neck. The low rumble grew to a steady growl, and two bright narrow eyes stared at her from across the room. She gulped and slowly shone her flashlight beam into the far corner.

12

More Pieces Turn Up

"What is that?" George asked, moving back against the stairway wall.

The rumbling growl continued. Clayton inched his way back down the steps. "It's over there," Nancy said. "Move your light slowly. I don't want to startle whatever it is."

The two beams slowly converged on the corner. There was a slight rustling sound, and the growling animal stood up as the light shone on it.

"It's a dog," George whispered. "Or is it?"

"It's a coyote. Right, Clayton?" Nancy said, her voice low.

"Yep," Clayton said, his voice husky. "And remember what I said about the danger when a coyote feels trapped."

Nancy heard the anxiety in Clayton's voice and felt a chill slip down her spine. The coyote inched forward, then back, then forward again. Its lips were curled back as it growled, showing rows of pointed yellow teeth.

"We've got to get out of here," Clayton said.

"Let's back up the stairs slowly," Nancy said. "Keep the lights aimed on the coyote."

"And no sudden moves," Clayton added. "Watch your step. We don't want anyone falling."

As the three stepped back up the steps, the coyote continued its threatening dance. Forward, backward, forward again. The farther up they went, the closer the coyote moved.

Finally Nancy felt the door against her back. She leaned on it, but it was just as Clayton had said—it gave a little, but wouldn't open.

"I think there's something jammed against it," Nancy murmured. She remembered the scraping sound she had heard before the door was slammed shut. She visualized the furniture on the first floor of the old farmhouse. "It must be that cabinet that was in the dining room. That's the only thing I can think of that would be heavy enough."

"It's pretty big, but I think we can move it, if we work together," Clayton said, his voice low.

"Uh, folks," George said. "Let's not forget Fido here. He's getting closer."

George was right. With all its pacing and stepping, the coyote had gotten bolder. Now it was crouched at the foot of the stairway.

"Take my light," Nancy said, handing it to George. "I have something in my pack that might do the trick. Although I hoped I wouldn't need it." Slowly, with no sudden moves, Nancy slid her pack off her arm and unzipped it. She reached into the pack and pulled out two large rawhide chew bones, which she held behind her back.

"Whoa," Clayton said, with a smile. "Are those from my grocery bag?"

"Mm-hmm," Nancy said. "With all that talk about coyotes in the Badlands, I thought I'd better slip a couple in my pack just in case."

"If it's good enough for Brutus, it should be good enough for this guy," George muttered.

"Just ease it on down the steps," Clayton advised. "Pull your hand around slowly."

Nancy gently rolled one of the bones down the stairs. At first, the coyote seemed startled and looked as if it were going to pounce. Then it backed off as the bone rolled its way.

Nancy held her breath. The bone stopped on the bottom step. The coyote came back out of the shadows and sniffed the chew toy. Then in one quick movement, it grabbed the bone in its mouth and backed off into the shadows.

Relieved, Nancy heard the unmistakable sounds of gnawing coming from the dark corner.

"Okay," Clayton said. "Let's get out of here. We don't have long."

"George, let's all help push," Nancy said.

They lined up in front of the door and jammed their shoulders against the wood. A grinding scrape from the other side of the door indicated some success. The door opened enough so that they could see light from the living room.

"Again," Nancy said. The second try opened the door enough that Nancy and George could slip through the opening. "Easy," Nancy whispered. "We don't know what—or who—we're going to find."

There was no one in sight. Together, Nancy and George moved the large, heavy cabinet farther away so Clayton could come through the opening. As they slowly moved the cabinet away, Nancy noticed a scrap of paper on the floor.

Finally Clayton was able to get out of the basement. He leaned against the wall and dropped to a crouch. "Whew," he said, his breath coming out with a whoosh. "That's as close as I *ever* want to get to a coyote."

Nancy reached down and picked up the scrap of paper and put it in her pocket. "Let's get out of here," she said, heading for the door.

"What about our friend down there?" Clayton said. "Should we close the basement back up?"

"No," Nancy said. "Let's take our cue from Ms. Francoeur and let him run free." She threw another chew bone so it rested at the open basement door. "Here's a little encouragement."

They hurried to the front door. Nancy looked

outside, but saw no one. "Come on," she said. "Let's get back to the car. But stay down. Whoever locked us in might still be around."

They darted to the fence and back to the car. "At last," George said. "Let's get out of here."

Clayton turned the car around and they were soon on the road back to the Turner ranch. George turned around to face Nancy and said, "You picked up something from the floor when we were moving the cabinet. What was it?"

Nancy reached in her pocket and pulled out the scrap of paper. "It was under the cabinet," she said. "It looks like part of a card of some kind—a membership card, maybe."

George and Clayton looked at the paper lying in Nancy's palm. "See?" Nancy said. "There's some sort of an embossed seal here."

"There are some words," George said, "parts of words anyway." She examined the card. Then she read off the word fragments. "One line has 'ure,' the next line has 'ine,' and the last line has 'ors.' What could they be?"

"We'll check when we get to the ranch," Nancy said. "The library can help, or the Internet."

"So you think it might have been dropped by the bad guys?" Clayton asked.

"Probably," Nancy said. "We did a thorough search before we went into the basement. Did either of you notice it then?" Both Clayton and George shook their heads. "I didn't either," Nancy said. "So one of them must have dropped it."

"You do think there was more than one?" Clayton asked.

"Yes," Nancy said. "That cabinet was really heavy. It would take two to move it."

On the way back to the ranch, they made one small detour so Nancy could drop off her film at a drugstore with one-hour developing service. By the time they got home, it was six-thirty. The Turners and Bess were sitting down to supper.

Nancy, George, and Clayton took their seats. "How is the sheriff?" Nancy asked.

"He's going to be fine," Mrs. Turner said, setting plates and napkins for Nancy, George, and Kincaid. "We talked to him on the phone about a half hour ago. The bullet went clean through and missed all his vital organs. It'll take a little time to heal, but he should be okay."

"No thanks to Badger Brady and his worthless family," Mr. Turner said, slamming his coffee mug down on the table. Drops of coffee spurted onto the green-checked tablecloth. "They've launched a manhunt for the whole gang," he continued. "I'd like to get Badger alone for a few minutes. I'd make him sorry he ever came back to South Dakota."

"Well, I hope that never happens. And I hope he doesn't come back to our place," Kincaid said. "He's like a loose cannon." She turned to Clayton. "So, how was your day, old buddy?" she asked.

"We had a pretty wild time at the Badlands," Clayton said.

Nancy, Clayton, and George told the Turners about

113

the probable poachers. Then Nancy decided to tell them they had gone to Badger Brady's.

"What!" Mr. Turner said. "You actually went there and got inside that rustler's house?"

"That was pretty dangerous," Mrs. Turner said. "It's a wonder you didn't get into trouble."

"Well, actually . . ." Clayton began. Then they told the Turners and Bess about the coyote.

"Yikes!" Bess said. "Usually, I'm sorry to miss one of Nancy's adventures, but I think I'm happy I passed on that one."

Nancy pulled out the fragment of paper she had found under the heavy cabinet.

"You know what this might be," Mr. Turner said, looking at the paper scrap, "it could be a union card. See these little letters here around that seal? They're pretty messed up and can't really be read. But they remind me of union membership cards I've seen."

"Good idea," Nancy said. "Thanks."

"By the way, Nancy," Mrs. Turner said. "Jack Allbright called. He did paint the illustration for the Justice for Animals brochure. He said Antoinette Francoeur fixed him up with some local animals for models. He said to give him a call if you need any more information." She handed Nancy a paper with the artist's phone number on it.

After dinner, everyone helped clean up. Then Clayton left, saying he'd had enough for one day.

Kincaid's parents went to the hospital to visit

Sheriff Switzer while Nancy, Bess, George, and Kincaid went back to the guest cabin.

Bess booted up Kincaid's laptop computer and logged on to the Internet. She checked several sites about labor unions. Finally she checked a list of local labor organizations for a union name that might include the syllables *ure, ine,* and *ors.* Scanning down the list, she found only one that fit: Moving Pic*ture* Mach*ine* Opera*tors.*

"What are those? The guys who run the movies in a theater?" Kincaid asked.

"Must be," Nancy said. "We'll call the local chapter tomorrow to make sure. But they're probably projectionists in movie theaters. I also want to find out if there's any chance Badger Brady is a member of that union."

The four sat in front of the fire and talked about the case. "I want to know who locked us in the basement," George said. "The way I see it, there are three possibilities: Badger Brady, the two men we saw in the Badlands, or total strangers."

"I really don't think it was Badger Brady," Nancy said. "Especially if he was by himself. That cabinet is just too heavy."

"Don't forget Miss Francoeur was in the area," George said. "Could she and one of her henchmen have done it?"

"Not likely," Nancy said. "How would she have known we were there? Besides, she would have liberated the coyote first. It could have been the

115

guys from the Badlands, though," Nancy said. "They may have seen our license plate when we drove away. They saw me talking on the phone, so they probably figured we were calling the ranger station. Maybe they followed us to Badger's and locked us in the basement so we wouldn't identify them."

"But you took their picture," Bess said.

"Yes, but they don't know that," Nancy pointed out. "When they looked up, I was holding the binoculars. They never saw my camera."

"It still could be the total strangers theory," George pointed out. "Someone who was using the house and was surprised to find us there. Maybe even some of Brady's family."

"I don't think that works, either," Nancy said. "After all, we were trespassing. They could have kicked us out. Why lock us up—especially if they knew about our roommate in the basement? It seems pretty extreme."

"Hey, guys," Kincaid said. "I hate to say this, but what has all this got to do with Lulu and Justice? We seem to be way off track here."

"It seems that way, doesn't it?" Nancy said. "If I could just find out who made the threatening call. After our confrontation at the Stomp, I'm pretty sure it wasn't Badger Brady." She took out the scrap of paper she'd found at Brady's ranch. "And if I could just figure out who locked us in the basement—and why." She stared at the paper.

"It's like we're putting a jigsaw puzzle together,"

she continued, frowning. "There are so many pieces. And none of them seems to fit. For example, there's that guy who knocked you down on the path at Mount Rushmore, Kincaid."

"You thought he might have recognized her," George said. "Too bad we couldn't really see him in the dark."

"Right," Nancy said. "I could tell he was tall, slim, and had light-colored hair. Well, one of the guys at the Badlands was tall, slim, and had gray hair."

"Maybe I'd recognize him if I could see his face," Kincaid said. "Let's get those photos!"

Kincaid pulled up to the drugstore drive-in window, and Nancy paid the clerk and then opened the envelope of photographs. She had ordered a double set of prints so she'd have extras to send to the Badlands rangers. Quickly, she shuffled through them until she got to the shots of the Badlands.

There were only two pictures, but both were very clear and close, thanks to the zoom lens. Instantly, Nancy remembered that moment when the man looked up from his digging. She remembered the feeling of his eyes boring into hers through the binoculars. She thought of the rage in his expression, and an icy chill cascaded down her arms.

"Wait a minute," Kincaid said, grabbing one of the photos from Nancy's hand. "I know him. That's Jasper Stone!"

13

Peril in the Pines

"Jasper Stone!" Nancy said, studying the photograph. "You mean the man who was an instructor when you were a summer intern?"

"Yeah," Kincaid said, her eyes blazing. "The poacher who stole the jawbone from my dig. Wow! It's kind of a shock seeing him in this photo." She passed the photo to Bess and George in the backseat.

"Looks like he hasn't changed his activities much either," George said.

"So he did recognize you on that path at Mount Rushmore," Bess said.

"No, not *him*," Kincaid said. "The other one. I don't know who the tall gray-haired guy is."

"Jasper Stone is the *other* one," Nancy said softly, staring at the photo.

When they got back to the ranch, Kincaid called Clayton and told him about the photos. "He offered to take the prints out to the Badlands tomorrow," Kincaid told Nancy. "He says he can tell them what he knows about Jasper Stone. It might help them track him down."

"Let's start early tomorrow," Nancy said. "First, I want to call the union about Badger Brady—*and* Jasper Stone. If neither of them is a projectionist, I want to check out all the movie theaters in the area. We can show them this photo. Maybe the other guy dropped the scrap of paper."

"That's a lot to do before lunch with Miss Francoeur," Bess said.

"And don't forget," George said. "You promised to take us back to Mount Rushmore tomorrow evening, Kincaid. And this time we're going as tourists. We're going to see the lighting show and everything."

"I remember," Kincaid said. "And I'm looking forward to it. But now, I'm exhausted." Kincaid left, and Nancy, Bess, and George fell into their beds for well-deserved sleep.

Thursday morning was gray and cool, with a soft light rain that misted the landscape. Nancy called the South Dakota chapter of the Moving Picture Machine Operators labor organization. They confirmed that it was a union for movie projectionists. They also told her they had never had a member named Badger Brady or Jasper Stone.

After breakfast Kincaid drove Nancy, Bess, and George to each of the four movie theaters in the area. Nancy talked her way into the offices and questioned the managers. None had ever employed a projectionist who looked like Jasper Stone or the other man in the Badlands photos.

Disappointed, the four girls went to RuthAnn's Tea Room to wait for Antoinette Francoeur. At fifteen minutes past one, there was a rustle as the Frenchwoman swept in. She was dressed in green gauze pants and tunic with navy blue embroidery. Her feet were strapped into sandals. Long gold-and-blue stone earrings dangled from her ears. When she was ushered to their table, Nancy braced herself.

"Oh no!" Ms. Francoeur said in her trumpeting voice. "It is you! My trespassers!" It seemed as if she would turn and stalk out.

"Ms. Francoeur, please wait," Nancy said, standing. She knew she had to appear very apologetic to spark the woman's curiosity. "We really need your help. Please talk with us."

Antoinette Francoeur's eyes narrowed as she studied Nancy. Nancy held her ground and never looked away. She didn't even blink.

Ms. Francoeur studied the other three. Finally

she let out a long sigh. "You have fifteen minutes," she said, waggling her finger at Nancy. "If I don't like what you say, I leave."

"Fair enough," Nancy said. "Shall we all order lunch first?"

"You talk first," Ms. Francoeur said. "I may not have the stomach for lunch."

Nancy, George, Bess, and Kincaid ordered sandwiches and lemonade. Nancy ordered an extra lemonade. "Just in case you get thirsty," she told Ms. Francoeur.

Nancy flashed the woman the sweetest smile she could manage. She could feel that their guest was very skittish. If Nancy asked the wrong question or disturbed her in any way, the woman would be out of there in a flash. Nancy resolved to take advantage of her opportunity.

After introductions, Nancy began, "How is your organization shaping up—Justice for Animals? It is such a worthy cause, of course."

"Is that really why we are here?" Ms. Francouer asked, studying Nancy carefully. "Are you all really going to start a young adult organization? Or was that merely a ruse to gain some time with me? And if so, for what purpose?"

Nancy took a deep breath. The woman was very defensive and suspicious. But she also seemed to enjoy turning the questioning back on Nancy.

"We certainly have talked about a young adult animal protection league," Nancy said. "We also wanted some time with you." She was pleased to see Ms. Francoeur take a long swallow of lemonade and call the waitress over.

After ordering a cheese tart and a plate of fruit, Ms. Francoeur turned to Kincaid. "Don't I know you?" she asked. "You are with the bison ranch. You show your animals in competitions?"

"That's right," Kincaid said.

"Mmmm," Ms. Francoeur murmured. Then she turned back to Nancy.

"Speaking of bison, Jack Allbright tells us you helped him find local animals to model for the brochure illustration."

Antoinette Francoeur seemed embarrassed. When her order arrived, she held up her hands, saying, "I am no longer hungry. Take it away."

Then she turned to Nancy. "You do not want to know just about my organization, am I right?" she said, leaning back in her seat, her arms crossed in front of her. "You have other questions burning your brain. Why don't you ask them."

"All right, I will," Nancy said, scooting forward to the edge of her seat. "Why didn't you call the sheriff or a guard when you found us in your auto barn? Why did you just let us go?"

Ms. Francoeur's eyes lit up with surprise. She looked intently at Nancy. "Why, I . . . I didn't want to get you in trouble," she said. "My automobiles are very famous. People wander in there. I do not have them arrested for it."

She folded and unfolded her napkin several

times. Nancy could tell this was a question the woman had not expected. Nancy continued quickly. "We saw a truck in your auto barn. It had very distinctive hubcaps."

"And what of it?" Ms. Francoeur said. "They are custom-made by a friend."

Nancy told the woman about the hubcap found near Lulu and Justice's trashed shelter. At this point, Kincaid seemed to explode with emotion. "Please, Ms. Francoeur, tell me the truth," she pleaded. "Did you take my bison? Where are they?"

The shock in Antoinette Francoeur's eyes seemed genuine. "I did not take them," she said. "I did not!" She looked at Nancy, then at Kincaid again. "Believe me, I did not take your animals."

"Were you on her ranch?" Nancy asked.

"Yes," Ms. Francoeur sputtered. "I heard you had isolated bison for grooming and training. I always worry when some of my animal friends are penned up. I drove out to check on them."

"And then what?" Nancy asked.

"I saw they were fed and sheltered," the Frenchwoman said. "They had enough water. They were as well as bison who are not free can be."

She looked down at the table. "And . . . well . . . they were perfect subjects for my illustration. They were easy to paint precisely because they were isolated. My artist could be close to them without being confronted by the rest of a herd. I picked up Jack and took him out there the next day. He spent an hour making sketches and taking photos. We would have stayed longer, but we saw a truck approaching across the pasture." She motioned to the waitress to bring back her lunch.

"I assumed it was people from your ranch," Ms. Francoeur continued. "Jack and I escaped quickly—so quickly I banged a rock as we drove off. That is probably when I lost the hubcap."

Kincaid's eyes were filled with tears. Ms. Francoeur seemed sympathetic. "I am so sorry to hear your bison are missing. Believe me, please. They were fine when we left."

They all picked at their food. Nancy knew that Kincaid was hoping the Frenchwoman had taken Lulu and Justice. And she was also counting on getting them back. Now, no one knew where they were.

Was Ms. Francoeur telling the truth? Nancy wondered. Or was it a well-played act to hide the fact that she had indeed taken Lulu and Justice?

"By the way," Nancy said, "I understand you were in the Badlands yesterday."

"I was," the woman answered. "We were there to see if the parade of tourists is disturbing the native animals in the Badlands." She stabbed a strawberry with her fork. "I am leaving now," she said. "Thank you for my lunch." She stood and glided away, with no further word.

Nancy and the others talked about their conversation with the eccentric Frenchwoman and concluded that she seemed to be telling the truth.

After they left RuthAnn's Tea Room, they ran the few errands that Kincaid had promised her parents. By then, it was time to head out of town and up into the Black Hills again.

Nancy could tell Kincaid was depressed about Lulu and Justice, but was trying not to let it ruin their afternoon.

"We don't have to see the Mount Rushmore show tonight," Bess said gently, as Kincaid started the drive up the mountain.

"No, I'd like to," Kincaid said. "It's really exciting. And it'll help take my mind off Lulu and Justice. I've almost given up ever seeing them again. I might as well face up to it."

Nancy's heart ached for her friend. She searched her brain as they rode, going over all the clues again and again. She felt as if her mind was just going in circles.

"I've already told Nancy and George a little about the show," Bess said. "But not everything. I want them to be as thrilled as I was when I first saw it."

Kincaid and Bess guided Nancy and George around the visitor center complex. They toured the preserved studio of Gutzon Borglum, who spent the last thirteen years of his life carving the presidents' heads. They had supper in the restaurant and spent nearly an hour in the gift shop.

Finally, it was time for the show. Nancy, George, Bess, and Kincaid took their seats on a wooden bench in the amphitheater. When everyone was seated, it was almost dark, and the sculptures across the canyon were nearly invisible.

Then music echoed through the canyons. A voice began narrating the history of the famous carvings, which were begun in 1927. While the narrator spoke, lights went up on a flat plane of granite that served as a movie screen. A film illustrating the narration began.

"Of course!" she whispered to Bess, George, and Kincaid. "It's a movie! And it must have a projectionist. We'll stay after the show to see if we can spot our man."

"All the lights go off for a few minutes after the film," Kincaid explained in a low voice. "And it's pitch black."

"Then they suddenly shine spotlights on the sculptures and the music plays," Bess added. "It's so dramatic. I cried when I saw it last summer."

"Okay, we'll make our move when the movie ends and all the lights go out," Nancy told them. "Follow my lead. I'm going to head for the studio. We'll stay in the woods behind it."

The film was entertaining, but Nancy couldn't keep her attention on it. She kept waiting for the moment when all went dark. A keen alertness filled her body. She was ready to jump and run.

Finally that moment came—the end of the movie. As the music wound to a close, the lights went out. It was very dark. Nancy stepped quickly out of her row, the others following. They all darted up the aisle and out of the amphitheater.

By the time the music began again and the sculptures were bathed in spotlights and fireworks, Nancy and the others were concealed in a grove of spruce trees behind the sculptor's studio. It was the same path they had taken on Tuesday night on their way to Antoinette Francoeur's.

At last people began leaving the amphitheater heading toward the parking lot. Nancy and the others spotted their man, his cap pulled down over his face. He was moving up the path, favoring his right leg with a slight limp.

"Bess, you and Kincaid stay here," Nancy said. "If we all go after him, he's bound to hear us. You can be our lookouts." They waited until he passed, then Nancy aimed her flashlight at the ground, and she and George quietly stepped through the forest after the stranger.

At first he followed the same trail they had taken Tuesday night. But then he veered off to one side and plunged into the dark, dense forest. They walked past several Private Property signs.

They walked for about half an hour. Nancy tried to keep up with the stranger, but she lost sight of him. Wary of a trap, she moved carefully, closely followed by George. It was so dark. Only a few beams of moonlight filtered down through the sharp needles of the trees. Because of her flashlight, Nancy was afraid to follow too closely. She didn't want to call the stranger's attention to them. She stepped very carefully to avoid crunching the thick bed of pine needles on the trail.

Nancy motioned to George to stop next to a large fallen tree. They both stood very still. Nancy strained to hear, but there was no sound ahead. She gestured to George to stay down and be quiet. Then Nancy stepped cautiously forward.

She walked about forty yards up the rough trail, but saw no sign of him. Resigned, she doubled back to return to the fallen tree and George. When she had walked back about thirty yards, a shaft of moonlight pierced the curtain of branches. As it shone on the forest floor, Nancy felt uneasy. She knelt and looked at the path more closely. "Something's happened here," she murmured.

The pine needles had been pulled or pushed away from the dirt. It looked as if something had been dragged across the trail. Nancy's heart sank as she rushed to the fallen tree. "Oh no," she murmured. Broken branches and scattered pine needles indicated a struggle had taken place. Lying in the exposed dirt was George's sports watch, its band twisted and broken.

14

Finding the Mother Lode

Nancy twirled around. "George!" she called in a loud whisper. "George! Where are you?" She reached down to pick up her friend's watch and dropped it in her pocket.

There was no response, no sound at all. Nancy took out her flashlight and aimed it at the ground next to the fallen tree. There's definitely been a struggle here, she thought. Her heart pounded and, for a minute, she felt as if she couldn't breathe. No wonder I lost his trail, she thought. He must have doubled back and found George waiting here.

She flashed the light on the ground. The dragged pine needles led to the right, and Nancy followed that trail.

Within minutes she had stumbled into a clearing in front of a hill. If she hadn't followed the trail of dragged pine needles and dirt, she would never had found the spot. It was completely surrounded by trees and dense undergrowth. An opening was cut into the side of the hill.

Nancy aimed her flashlight beam into the opening and gasped. George lay on the ground. Her hands were tied behind her back. Her ankles were bound together, and she lay very still.

Nancy rushed through the opening. "George!" she called. "Say something! Are you all right?"

Nancy put her flashlight on the ground and knelt beside her friend. George's pulse was steady, but she was knocked out cold. Nancy slipped off her backpack and took out her flashlight and a bottle of water.

She aimed the flashlight at George, then lifted her head and poured a little water on her lips. At first the water dribbled down George's chin. Then she sputtered and coughed. Her eyes blinked open, and they widened with fear as she peered over Nancy's shoulder.

"Ach, you found us at last," a man muttered behind Nancy. "Welcome."

Nancy whipped her head around to see a short stocky man slam a wooden door down over the opening. Nancy laid George back down and moved to the door. It was solid and didn't budge when she pushed on it.

Nancy went back to George. "The door is locked or jammed shut somehow," she said, untying the knots on George's wrists. "What happened?"

"I don't really know," George said, rubbing her wrists. "I sat waiting for you, and the next thing I knew I was in here waking up." She reached up and touched the back of her head. "Yow, that hurts," she said, rubbing her head.

"He must have knocked you out," Nancy said. "I didn't see who locked us in very clearly. But I recognized the voice. It was the same man who made the threatening call to the Turners' Monday night." She untied George's ankles. "And he appeared to be the same shape and size as Jasper Stone."

"So it wasn't the guy we were following?" George asked, slipping off her backpack.

"Nope," Nancy said, sweeping her light around the small room. "But they're clearly partners in crime."

George turned on her flashlight and swung it around. "Looks like a mine of some kind," she said. "Maybe gold. Kincaid said there used to be a lot of gold found around here. Maybe we've stumbled on an abandoned mine."

Nancy walked toward the back of the room. An arched opening led to another room. "There's a larger room back here," she said. "Maybe there's another way out." She flashed her light around the second room. "Whoa—there's something in here."

She stepped carefully into the second room. "George! Come here," Nancy gasped. "You're not going to believe this!"

George hurried over, and her light joined Nancy's to illuminate the second room. Several stacks of bones lined the room. Massive skulls and feet, huge curved tusks, bones longer than Nancy was tall. All were obviously from another time.

A cool shiver rippled through Nancy as she gazed at the eerie sight. "We've stumbled onto something big, George," she said. "Somebody's been stashing prehistoric fossils here."

"Poachers, right?" George asked. "Why else would bones be stashed in such a remote place?"

"Exactly," Nancy said. "If they were legitimate, why lock us in here?"

"Speaking of which," George said, "let's get out. I'd love to look at all these bones. But I'd rather not do it as a prisoner."

Nancy and George went back to the door. They both pushed with all their strength but couldn't budge it. "Easy, George," Nancy said. "You need to rest. You might still be a little groggy from the blow to your head. Besides, I hear something banging against the door each time we push," Nancy said. "I have a feeling it's a padlock."

"We're sunk," George said.

"Don't give up yet," Nancy said. "Let's look around." The two flashed their beams around the room, over the floor, around the walls, and across the ceiling. Nancy went into the second room. As she swept her light across the floor, she noticed a couple of pieces of charred wood in the far corner. She picked one up. It was so old it crumbled into black dust when she touched it.

She flashed her light around and found more in the same area. "Look," she said, pointing them out to George. "And look here." She crouched in the area where the charred wood was scattered. The ground dipped into a shallow hollow there.

"What is it?" George asked.

"This looks as if someone had fires here a long time ago," Nancy said. "Maybe when this was a real mine. South Dakota winters can be horrible. They had to keep warm while they worked."

"So?" George said.

"So they had to have some kind of vent for the smoke," Nancy said, standing up. She moved the beam of light back and forth across the ceiling. Finally, she found an area that seemed to be darker than the rest of the ceiling.

She looked around for a stick or a branch. There was nothing but bones. She prodded at them until she found what she wanted. "How are you feeling?" she asked, rolling out a bone nearly seven feet long. "Can you give me a hand?"

"I'm feeling okay," George said. "You know me. Whatever it takes to get out of here." Nancy thought of all of George's athletic achievements. She was sure her friend could handle this, too.

Together, they held the long bone upright and poked at the ceiling where Nancy saw the darkened area. Showers of black powder fell on their faces. Nancy rubbed some of it off her cheek and smelled it. "Soot," she said, with a grin. "Come on. There must be an opening up there somewhere."

Nancy and George hoisted the prehistoric bone, jamming it into the ceiling of the room. Clumps of dirt pummeled them from above, then splinters of wood.

"I'll bet there's a trapdoor up there," Nancy said when the bits of wood began falling. "The miners probably opened it as a vent when they built a fire. Keep pounding."

At last, the bone seemed to break through to another level. Dirt and roots rained down on them, then pine needles. "We're through," George cried, as Nancy felt the bone move up with no resistance.

"Okay, now what?" George said, as they looked at the hole seven and a half feet above the floor.

"How about this?" Nancy asked. She tugged at an enormous skull lying against the wall. She and George were able to roll it across the floor to a spot beneath the vent in the ceiling. "We don't know who—or what—might be out there," Nancy warned. "I'll go first. Wait until I signal."

Nancy climbed onto the skull and was able to get her head and shoulders through the opening in the ceiling. She hoisted herself up and out.

"Okay, I'm clear," she whispered through the vent back to George. "Wait while I check the front door. Maybe I can pick the lock."

"No way," George said. "I'm out of here." And she popped up through the trapdoor.

They were on top of the small hill that the mine cut through. After scrambling down the hill, they followed the trail made by George's dragged body back to the fallen tree. They stayed hidden in the forest and didn't talk, in case their captors were still around. Finally, they reached the Private Property signs they had passed before. Then they crossed back into the federal land that surrounded the Mount Rushmore Memorial.

After another half hour, they rejoined Bess and Kincaid, who were frantic. "What happened to you?" Bess asked.

Nancy imagined how she must look—soot on her face, weeds and pine needles in her hair. "We'll talk on the way. We have to find a ranger—quick!"

The four walked back down the nature path to the Mount Rushmore Visitor Center. On the way, Nancy and George related what had happened.

When they reached the visitor center plaza, they saw a ranger standing on one of the terraces. "Good," Kincaid said under her breath. "I've met her before with Clayton. Maybe we won't get into too much trouble sneaking around after hours."

She walked up to the ranger. "Hi," she said with a winning smile. "I'm Kincaid Turner. I met you once with Clayton Simmons. His dad's a ranger here, too—Hillard Simmons."

The ranger frowned at them. "I know Clayton

and his dad," she said. "I don't know you. And I sure don't know what you're doing here after hours." She spoke into her walkie-talkie and another ranger soon joined them.

When the second ranger arrived, Kincaid introduced herself again. Then she introduced Nancy, Bess, and George. Before the two rangers could get another word out, Nancy and Kincaid began telling their story.

They related their first experience here with the man on the trail. Then they told about the poachers at the Badlands and showed the rangers the photos. Nancy showed them the scrap of union card. Kincaid explained that they wanted to set up a sting to catch the possible poacher here. Then Nancy and George told what had just happened to them.

The ranger called Clayton's dad. "He wants to speak to you," she said to Kincaid.

"Ranger Simmons, we really need your help," Kincaid said. She listened for a minute, then said to Nancy, "He's completely up to speed. Clayton told him everything." Then she spoke back into the phone. "We're sure we've found poachers' fossils," she said, "and if someone doesn't get out there quick, they're going to lose the men and their hoard. We think one of them works here."

Ranger Simmons vouched for Kincaid and her friends to the other rangers and said he'd be right out with more men. Kincaid, Nancy, and George used a map to trace a rough path to the abandoned mine.

"And you'll let us know what happens in your investigation?" Nancy asked as the rangers prepared to leave for the mine.

"Yes, we will," one of the rangers assured her. "Now, I suggest you leave here and get back home as quickly as possible. When that man finds you've escaped and can identify him, you could be in danger." The girls hurried to their car.

"George, how are you feeling?" Nancy asked. "Do you think you should get checked over?"

"Nah, I'm fine," George said. "I feel like Bess did when she nearly fell off the mountain. Just lead me to that shower and bed."

"One thing I don't understand," Bess said. "How come those guys used a mine cave so close to the memorial?"

"It's on private property," Nancy said. "Maybe they own it. It's almost an hour's walk from the memorial and completely hidden and surrounded by trees and undergrowth. The opening is camouflaged in the side of a hill. If I hadn't followed the trail of dragged pine needles, I'd never have found it."

"So how did they get the bones in there?" George asked.

"Because it's private property," Nancy said, "we don't know what kind of roads might be back in there on the rest of the land."

"They had to have some way of getting the gold out at one time," Bess said, nodding.

"Matt's out of the hospital—we'll call him from

the ranch," Kincaid said. "It's after midnight. If I know Clayton's dad, he's probably called my folks and told them what's happened. They're going to worry until they see me home safe and sound."

Kincaid drove back to the ranch in record time. When they arrived, Melissa Turner ran out to meet them. "Hillard Simmons called us," she said, running to the car. "George, how are you?"

"I'm okay, Mrs. Turner," George said, with a lopsided smile. "Really."

When they walked into the kitchen, Mr. Turner was seated at the table with Sheriff Switzer. The sheriff had his arm in a sling. "Matt, you didn't have to come out," Kincaid said. "We were going to call you as soon as we got in."

"I called Matt before we heard about your trouble," Mr. Turner said. "We just had twelve more bison stolen!"

15

All the Pieces Fit

"No!" Kincaid said, tears welling in her eyes. "Twelve more?" She turned to the sheriff.

"We just can't seem to get a handle on this thing," the sheriff said, rubbing his shoulder. "There were tracks out there that made a pretty good match with the ones you lifted near Lulu's shelter," he added. "But we can't match them up with anything around here or on file with the FBI. They don't match Badger Brady's. We know that."

"What about that gang from Canada you mentioned?" Nancy asked.

"That's not panning out," Mr. Turner said. His elbows were on the table, and he held his head in his hands. "If we don't get this solved pretty soon, I don't know what I'm going to do. This last bunch included some of my best breeding stock."

"How about Ms. Francoeur?" Bess asked. "Did you ask her about the hubcap?"

"Yes," the sheriff replied. He told them what the Frenchwoman had said. It was the same story she had told Nancy and her friends at the tearoom, and they all agreed it was probably true.

"Well, we have a new truck for you to check," Nancy said. She could see in her mind the license plate of the truck in the Badlands.

"Sit, everyone," Mrs. Turner said, pouring coffee and tea. "I want to hear what happened to the girls tonight. Matt, I think you'll have a whole new case on your hands when you hear this."

When everyone was seated around the kitchen table, Nancy and her friends retold the entire story. Then Nancy showed Sheriff Switzer the photographs. "I recognize Jasper Stone all right," he said. "We've had trouble with him before. I didn't know he was back in town. The other guy's a new one on me. But I'll check with the rangers at Rushmore and the Badlands tomorrow."

"I've got major work myself tomorrow," Mr. Turner said, running his hand through his dark hair. "I've got to round up some more hands and pull the herd in even closer."

"You did that once, didn't you?" Nancy asked.

"Yep," Mr. Turner said, nodding. "But it wasn't close enough. It looks like I need to get them practically in the backyard to keep whoever it is from picking them off."

"Well, you girls have had another big day," Mrs. Turner said. "Why don't we all go to bed. George, I really think you need some rest. Tomorrow we can all start fresh."

As they walked to the guest house, Nancy, Bess, and George were quiet. Nancy was frustrated. She felt as if she was working from both ends of a puzzle and couldn't get it to meet in the middle. That night, she had a hard time sleeping. She tossed and turned while her mind worked.

Friday morning was sunny with a wide blue sky and tumbleweed clouds. Nancy, Bess, and George dressed quickly in jeans, shirts, and boots and hurried to the ranch house to meet Kincaid. Mrs. Turner offered the girls some breakfast, but Nancy shook her head. "I have an idea," she said.

"It must be a good one," Bess said, "if you can brush off one of Mrs. Turner's doughnuts."

"Well, what is it?" George asked. "Spill it."

"What if the buffalo rustling isn't the point at all?" Nancy suggested.

"What do you mean?" Kincaid said. "How could that be?"

"What if it's just a ploy—a diversion?" Nancy said.

"A diversion!" Kincaid repeated.

"Something to keep all of you busy and distract

141

you from what's really happening," Nancy said. "And especially to keep you away from remote areas of the ranch."

"I don't get it," Kincaid said.

"When the buffalo are rustled, your father's response is to pull the herd in closer, right?" Nancy said.

"Right," Kincaid said.

"Suppose something's going on at a remote area of your ranch," Nancy suggested. "Something secret. And the best way to keep it secret is to keep all of you away from that area and so busy trying to solve one problem that you don't realize what's really going on."

Kincaid looked at Nancy and her eyes seemed to glow like spotlights. "A dig," she whispered. "Oh, Nancy, that's it!"

"A dig?" George said. "On the ranch?"

"Of course," Bess said, jumping up. "Think, Kincaid. Where are your secret spots? Are there any you haven't visited for a while?"

"Sure," Kincaid said. "Several."

Nancy grabbed a doughnut and headed for the door. "Come on, everybody. Let's go take a look."

At that moment the phone rang. It was Sheriff Switzer. Mrs. Turner switched the call to the speaker phone. "I talked to the rangers at Rushmore and the Badlands," the sheriff said. "The second man in Nancy's photo was Ephraim Tell. He and Jasper Stone have a reputation with the FBI as criminal archaeological poachers. Stone owns the property that the abandoned mine is on."

"Have they arrested them?" Mrs. Turner asked.

"The Mount Rushmore rangers found the mine and the fossils, but there was no sign of the two men. Since Nancy thought they might have been the ones who followed her and the others to Badger Brady's and locked them in the basement, I had them check out there, too. But they weren't there, either. Neither was the coyote, by the way."

Kincaid sighed, saying, "Where *are* they?"

"We'll find them," Sheriff Switzer said. "At least now we know who we're looking for. Oh, and Badger Brady has been arrested. He was picked up in Kansas. They're bringing him back tomorrow."

Nancy told the sheriff her theory about the men poaching on the Turners' land. "We know Jasper poached that jawbone from here years ago," she added. "We're going to take a look around."

"You be careful," the sheriff said. "Those guys might be dangerous. I'll be out with some men right away," he concluded before hanging up.

The girls raced to Kincaid's vehicle, as Mrs. Turner repeated the sheriff's warning.

"There are two possible spots," Kincaid said, as she took off across the pasture. "One of them is near where I found the jawbone. It's on the other side of the ranch. I haven't been there for a long time."

"Let's go there first," Nancy said. "We know Jasper has been there before."

As they neared the area, Nancy noticed Kincaid's fingers. They were gripping the steering wheel so tightly, her knuckles were white. "Kincaid, what is it?" Nancy asked.

"It's different," Kincaid said. "There used to be some shrubs here. And what's that building?"

Nancy and the others looked where Kincaid was pointing. There was a crudely built lean-to at the base of a hill. Kincaid parked the car, and they cautiously crept up to the shed. It was locked. Lying in the grass near the shed was a small pickax with the initials E.T. on it.

"Ephraim Tell," Bess said in a whisper.

"Come on," Kincaid said. Nancy and her friends followed Kincaid over the rise of a hill. "Whoa," Kincaid said. The side of the hill was completely veiled in a tarpaulin anchored to the ground with dozens of stakes roped together. George and Kincaid pulled up the stakes. Nancy and Bess rolled back the tarp.

There, embedded in the hill, was an enormous skeleton lying on its side. "It's a giant sea reptile!" Kincaid said. "I can't believe it. I've seen pictures of them, but never thought I'd ever be this close to one. They don't even have a name. It lived here when this spot was the bottom of a sea—over a hundred million years ago."

Bess put an arm around her friend's shoulder, saying, "Maybe they'll name it the *Kincaidosaurus* when you finish recovering it."

The sound of an approaching truck startled

them. The girls ran back around the hill in time to see a black truck wheel around with a screech of its brakes and head away from the dig.

"It's them—in the same truck we saw in the Badlands," Nancy said, racing to Kincaid's vehicle. "They must have just seen our car. Come on, they're getting away." Within minutes they were chasing the truck.

For a mile or two, they sped over open pastureland. "We need to trap them somehow," Nancy said. "Chase them into a holding area."

"I've got just the spot," Kincaid said. "We'll round 'em up like we do the bison." She maneuvered her car to the left, then to the right, forcing the driver of the truck to swerve away.

Nancy grabbed some binoculars off the floor of Kincaid's vehicle and peered at the occupants of the black truck. "It's them, all right," she said. "Tell's driving, Stone's the passenger. No one's aiming a gun this way. Pull up closer."

With a loud "Yeeeeah," Kincaid took out across the bumpy ground, her foot slamming down on the accelerator. She sidled her vehicle beside the truck and steered right, forcing Tell to make a wide curve. Then Kincaid moved around to the left, forcing Tell to come back to a straighter line.

"Yow," Bess said from the backseat. "This is worse than a roller coaster."

"Don't let them get away," George yelled.

Kincaid was right. It was like guiding an animal

herd. She wheeled from side to side, making sure her quarry was headed where she wanted.

"There they go!" she finally yelled, braking her car and turning it just in time.

The truck couldn't stop. It plummeted down a hill and into a shallow river that flowed through a narrow gorge. Nancy and the others ran to the edge of the gorge to check on the two men. When they got there, both men were lying on the shore, panting. The truck was badly damaged and sunk to the tops of its wheels in gooey mud.

"Jasper Stone, you crook," Kincaid yelled down. "You'll never poach from our land again!"

"My friend's leg," Stone called up. "I think it's broken."

"Is he conscious?" Nancy asked. "Are either of you bleeding?"

"No, but we are in pain," Stone replied, "and in need of assistance to get out of here."

"We'll get you some help," Kincaid said, "but first tell me about my bison. Have you rustled from our herd? Did you take my cow and her calf?"

"Ms. Turner, we'll tell you everything," Stone said. "But get us out of here."

"Not until you tell me where Lulu and Justice are," Kincaid said, her voice wild with anger. "They had better be all right."

"They're fine, okay?" Ephraim Tell yelled. "They're on my ranch, about forty miles from here. Now get me a doctor. My leg's killing me."

"Please, Ms. Turner," Stone said. "I assure you

my friend is telling the truth. We were never interested in your bison, just your fossils. Your animals are fine. Please get us out of here."

Nancy recognized the voice. "You made that threatening call to the Turners, didn't you?" she said. "I answered the phone, not Kincaid. And you locked my friend and me in the mine cave?"

"That's right," Stone said, as his partner groaned. "You were trespassing on my property."

"Just lie still, Mr. Tell," Nancy said. "Don't move your leg. Have you been working as a projectionist at Mount Rushmore?"

"Yeah, yeah, yeah," Tell answered. "Gave me a uniform, so I looked legit walking around the area. Gave me access to Stone's property and the cave without hauling up the logging roads."

"Just one more question," Nancy said. "Did you two follow us to the Brady farmhouse and lock us in the basement?"

Stone nodded, but didn't speak.

"With a coyote!" Kincaid said. "Nice going, Stone. We'll get help, but you don't deserve it."

"George and I will stay here and keep an eye on them," Nancy said. "They're really no threat. They can't climb up the cliff—they're stuck in the gorge until you bring some help."

Kincaid and Bess drove back to the ranch house to meet Sheriff Switzer. He and his men brought paramedics out to rescue the poachers and relieve Nancy and George of their watch.

* * *

The next day the sheriff, the FBI, Mr. Turner, and a few of his ranch hands followed Ephraim Tell's instructions and drove several livestock trailers out to Tell's ranch.

A few hours later Kincaid was pacing up and down the drive while Nancy, Bess, George, and Mrs. Turner sat on the porch and waited. "You're going to wear a hole in the ground," Bess warned, smiling at her friend.

"I know, but I can't wait," Kincaid said. "Lulu and Justice have to be okay. They *have* to."

At the sound of a car coming up the drive, Kincaid stopped pacing. "It's only Clayton," she said, her shoulders slumping when she saw him.

The girls quickly caught Clayton up on the day's events, and he joined the wait-and-watch for word from Ephraim Tell's ranch.

At last they all heard it—the distinctive rumble of a huge vehicle rolling up the drive. Mr. Turner pulled the livestock trailer to an expert halt and jumped out of the cab. Without a word, he and his ranch hands opened the back of the trailer and eased out a large chocolate brown bison cow and a cinnamon-colored calf.

"Lulu! Justice!" Kincaid howled. "You're back!" She threw her arms partway around Lulu's huge neck and nuzzled her face. Then she snuggled Justice close in her arms. "What did I tell you?" she said to the others, tears streaming down her cheeks. "Isn't he the most beautiful thing?"

"Matt and the FBI took custody of the rest of the

rustled herd," Bill Turner said, his arm wrapped tightly around Mrs. Turner's shoulders. "But he promised that after all the evidence is collected and checked, we'll get them back. It shouldn't be more than a few days. I told them that if I didn't bring Lulu and Justice home today, they'd have to answer to Kincaid."

Kincaid and her father walked the two bison to the corral, and everyone sat on logs watching Justice romp and nuzzle his mother.

"I'm glad it wasn't Antoinette Francoeur," Clayton said. "She's kind of nutty, but I like her anyway."

"I'm going to call her," Nancy said. "She seemed truly worried about Lulu and Justice. I think she'll like knowing they're okay."

"Nancy, we can't thank you enough," Kincaid said. "I was afraid I'd never see them again."

"You should have had more faith," Bess said with a laugh. "I told you that no one can buffalo Nancy Drew."

George groaned, then added, "Especially when she's so good at digging up clues!"

**Do your younger brothers and sisters
want to read books like yours?**

**Let them know there
are books just for *them*!**

They can join Nancy Drew and her best
friends as they collect clues and solve
mysteries in

THE
NANCY DREW
NOTEBOOKS®

Starting with

#1 The Slumber Party Secret

#2 The Lost Locket

#3 The Secret Santa

#4 Bad Day for Ballet

AND

**Meet up with suspense and mystery
in Frank and Joe Hardy:
The Clues Brothers™**

Starting with

#1 The Gross Ghost Mystery

#2 The Karate Clue

#3 First Day, Worst Day

#4 Jump Shot Detectives

Look for a brand-new story every
other month at your local bookseller

A MINSTREL® BOOK

Published by Pocket Books   1366-02

NANCY DREW® MYSTERY STORIES By Carolyn Keene

American S·I·S·T·E·R·S

Join different sets of sisters
as they embark on the varied,
sometimes dangerous,
always exciting journeys
that crossed America's landscape!

West Along the Wagon Road, 1852

A Titanic Journey Across the Sea, 1912

Voyage to a Free Land, 1630

Adventure on the Wilderness Road, 1775

By Laurie Lawlor

A MINSTREL BOOK

Published by Pocket Books

2030-01